Alexander Radcliffe

The Works of Capt. Alex. Radcliffe

In one volume: viz, Ovid's travestie, or, A burlesque upon Ovid's Epistles, likewise

his Ramble, an anti-heroick poem, with several miscellanies. Third Edition

Alexander Radcliffe

The Works of Capt. Alex. Radcliffe
In one volume: viz, Ovid's travestie, or, A burlesque upon Ovid's Epistles, likewise his Ramble, an anti-heroick poem, with several miscellanies. Third Edition

ISBN/EAN: 9783337213794

Printed in Europe, USA, Canada, Australia, Japan

Cover: Foto ©Andreas Hilbeck / pixelio.de

More available books at **www.hansebooks.com**

THE
WORKS
OF
Capt. *ALEX. RADCLIFFE*

In one Volume.
V I Z:

)vid's *Traveſtie :* Or a *Burleſque upon* O- vid's *Epiſtles.*		*Likewiſe his Ramble,* an *Anti-Heroick Po-* em, with ſeveral Miſ- cellanies.

The Third Edition Augmented.

L O N D O N,
rinted for *Richard Wellington* , at the *Lute* in St. *Paul's* Church-Yard. MDCXCVI.

TO

ROBERT FAIRBEARD

O F

GRAYS-INN, *Esquire.*

S I R,

Having committed these Epistles to the Press, *I* was horribly put to't for a Patron— *I* thought of some great Lord, or some Angelique Lady; but then again consider'd I should ever be able to adorn my Dedication with benign Beams, corus-ant Rays, and the Devil and all of Influence. At last I heard my

A 2   good

good *Friend* Mr. Fairbeard *was*
come to Town--nay then---all's wel*
enough. To you therefore I offer this
English Ovid, *to whom you may*
not be unaptly compar'd in several
parcels of your Life and Conversa
tion ; only with this exceptiou, Tha
you have nothing of his Triftibu*
you.

'Tis you who Burlesque all th*
Foppery and conceited Gravity
the Age. I remember yon once tol
a grave affected Advocate, That l
Burlesqu'd God's Image, for Go
had made him after his own Like
ness, but he made himself look li
an Ass.

The Epiſtle Dedicatory.

Upon the whole matter I am very well ſatisfi'd in my Choice of
you for my Judge; if you ſpeak
well of the Book, 'tis all I deſire,
and the Bookſeller will have reaſon
to rejoyce: tho' by your appaobation
you may draw upon your ſelf a grand
inconvenience; for perhaps you may
too often have Songs, Sonets, Madri-
als, and an innumerable Army of
Stanza's obtruded upon you by

Sir,

Octob, 28th.   Your humble Servant,
1680

Alex. Radcliffe.

A 3   TO

TO THE
READER.

Occasioned by the

PREFACE

To a late Book call'd

The WITS Paraphras'd.

BEfore I shall give you any Account of our Old Friend *Ovid,* or of his *Life*, I am to inform you, that his *Epistles* have been ingeniously and correctly translated by several Gentlemen; and withall, that he was of a good Family, and a brave Fellow was he.

Now,

Now, fince the unhappy Accident of his Death, his Ghoft has been lately attempted to be rais'd by an unlucky *Pretender* to *Poetry*, who indeed hath not skill enough to difturb his Manes: He calls his Book, *The Wits Paraphras'd*, or, *Paraphrafe upon Paraphrafe*, that is, *Throw, Pelion upon Offa, Offa upon Pelion*, and *away with it.* This Book he has dedicated to his Patron *Julian*, Secretary to the Mufes, in hopes that he may get and Under Writers Place fomewhere about *Pernaffus*: but alas! how can he ever hope for Preferment, when he has blafpheam'd the beft *Poets* of our Age, by miftaking *Innocence* for *Ignorance*: I wifh to God the laft may not rife up in Judgment againft him. He (good Soul) is (as appears in his Epiftle to his Patron) for none of your High Flights; but, like an humble Sinner in a ftrict Diet, makes all his *Similies* of *Cloofe-Stools* with *Velvet-Seats,* and *Pans* that receive the Excrement. God fave us: What are we when we are left to our felves.

Now

To the Reader.

Now for his *Preface*, he would imitate that ingenious one of Mr. *Dryden's* to *Ovid's Epistles*, in beginning with *Ovid's* Life, which hath been wrote by as many Men as there is *Lives* in *Plutarch*. And again, our *Paraphraser* faies, That *Ovid* was as good a Wit as Himself, or any other Translator ; and, to prove that, he faies, *Nescivit quod bene cessit*, &c. He might as aptly have said,

The Man in the Moon drinks Claret.

Then he faies, That he could find no such thing as *Clubbing* with *Ovid* in all the Catalogue of *Virgil*, *Catullus*, *Propertius* or *Tibullus :* very truly said : for I suppose he knows nothing farther of those Authors than the Catalogue.

Oh Tempor ! Oh Mores !
The more the merrier !

To the Reader.

He wonders, that so many Workmen should put their Shreds and Thrums together to dess *Ovid* in a *Buffoon's* Coat ! why a silly *Quaker*, in plain *Taunton* Serge, thinks a Scarlet Coat embroider'd to be the **Old** Serpent !

He questions not but that there are more Fools in the World of his Opinion. (The true Question is, whether he is not single ?)

Then he affirms, that, in his own simple naked shape, he comes nearer the Original, than the best of 'em ; when in *Sapho* to *Phaon* he begins at the sixth Distich, *Arva Phaon celebrat,* &c. and goes back to the fith, *Uror ut in Domitis*, &c. leaving out the eight Verses preceeding , by which you may easily guess that he had no other Authority for his *Paraphrase* (as he calls it) than the Translation : 'Tis something strange, that neither *Ovid* himself, nor Ninteen Judicious Translators, can give this Gentleman the least hint or light into *Publius Ovidius Naso's* meaning.

Quo

Quo te mori pedes ?———

Now on a sudden he's started from Poetry, and is possest with the Spirit of sublunary Wealth, and wishes with all his heart that he were as rich as a *M.* or a *C.* then would he quit all his title to P*ernaffus,* and engage never to write : oh, never to write any more, that is to say, he'd be so unconscionable as to have a good Estate for nothing :

God prospor long our Noble King———

Now, as he saies, the late Translators have already clipp'd the Original, and why should not he clip too: whereas my fear is, he hath clipp'd *Ovid* so close that it will hardly go :

When first King Henry, *&c.*

1

To the Reader.

I believe no Book hath had severer usage than our *Paraphrasers*; for saies he, it was hurry'd into the Press before it cou'd make any defence for it self: Now the meaning on't is, if it had met with impartial Judges, it had never been Printed.

The Glories of our Birth and State, &c.

But to conclude; Having wonderfully shew'd his Reading in his Preface to his aforesaid *Wits Paraphras'd*; in Scraps of old *Latin*; and at last, to his eternal Glory, one bit of false *Greek*; he is so far encourag'd, that he gives any man a Challenge in *Chaldee, Arabick,* and *Syriack*; though he confesses he knows nothing of the matter: But, to try him, I'll leave him with this *Syriack* Hexamiter.

Erytit ut ælutap snabucer bus enimget igaf.

And

To the Reader.

And to let you know that this laſt Verſe, though ſomething rough, is not the effect of Indignation, I part friendly; only with this Advice, That our *Paraphraſer* would conſider, and follow any other Employment, more agreeable with his Genius (if he have any) then that of Poetry.

THE

THE TABLE.

SAPHO

SAPHO to PHAON:

The ARGUMENT.

Sapho *was a Lady very Eminent for Singing of Bal-*
lads, and upon an a extraordinary Pinch, could
make one well enough for her Purpose : She held a
League with one Phaon, *who was her Companion*
and Partner in the Chorus *; but* Phaon *deserted*
his Consert for the Preferment of a Rubber in the
Ba'nnio. Sapho *took this so to heart, that she*
threatens to break her Neck out of a Garret Win-
dow ; which if effected, might proue her utter Destru-
Ction. Authors have not agreed concerning the ex-
ecution of her Design : But however she Writes him
this loving and terrifying Epistle.

W Hen these my doggrel Rhimes you chance (to see,

  You hardly will believe they came from (me,

T'ill you discover *Sapho's* Name at bottom,

You'l not imagine who it is that wrote 'em :

I, that have often Sung—*Young* Phaon *ſtrove*,
Now Sing this doleful Tune— *Farewel my Love*;
I muſt not Sing new Jiggs----the more's the Pity,
But muſt take up with ſome old Mournful Ditty.
You in the *Bannio* have a place, I hear;
I in my Garret Sweat as much, with Fear:
You can rub out a Living well enough,
My Rent's unpaid, poor *Sapho* muſt rub off;
My Voice is crack't, and now I only houl,
And cannot hit a Treble for my Soul:
My Ballads lye neglected on a Shelf,
I cannot bear the Burthen by my ſelf;
Doll Price the Hawker offers very fair,
She'l Sing along with me for Quarter-ſhare;
Sue Smith, the very ſame will undertake,
Their Voice is like the winding of a Jack.
Hang'em, I long to bear a Part with you,
I love to Sing, and look upon you too;

Beſides,

Besides, you know when Songs grow out of fashion,
That I can make a Ballad on occasion.

I'am not very Beautiful,——God knows;
Yet you should value one that can Compose:

Despise me not, though I'm a little Dowdy,
I can do that----same----like a bigger Body:

Perhaps you'l say I've but a tawny Skin;
What then? you know my Metal's good within.

What if my Shoulder's higher then my Head?
I've heard you say I'm Shape enough a-Bed:

The Mayor (God bless him) or the worthy Sheriffs
Do very often meet with homely Wives.

Our Master too; that little scrubbed Draper,
Has he not got a Lady that's a Strapper?

If you will have a Beauty, or have none,
Phaon must lye----*Phaon* must lye alone:

I can remember, 'fore my Voice was broke,
How much in praise of me you often spoke,

And

And when I fhook a Trill, you fhook your Ears,

And fwore I Sung like, what d'ee call'em--Spheres;

You kifs'd me hard, and call'd me Charming witch,

I can't do't now, if you wou'd kifs my Breach.

Then you not only lik'd my airy Voice,

But in my Flefhly part you did Rejoice ;

And when you clafp'd me in your brawny clutches,

You fwore I mov'd my Body like a Dutches ;

You clap'd my Buttocks, o're and o're agen,

I can't believe that I was crooked then.

Beware of him you Sifters of the quill,

That Sing at *Smithfield-Bars*, or *Saffron-Hill*,

Who, for an honeft Living, tear your Throat ;

If *Phaon* drinks w'ye you're not worth a groat:

And Ladies know, 'twill be a very hard thing

To fink from him the fmalleft Copper-farthing ;

Avoid him all —— for he has us'd me fo,

Wou'd make your hearts ake, if you did but know,

My

My Hair's about my Ears, as I'm a Sinner,
He has not left me worth a Hood or Pinner.
Phaon by me unworthily has dealt,
Has got my Ring,----though 'twas but Copper gilt ;
Yet that vexes me,----Th' ungrateful Pimp
Has ftole away my Peticoat with Gimp ;
Has all my Things, but had he left me any
I can't go out alone to get a Penny
Phaon I fhould have had lefs caufe to grieve,
If like a Man of Sence, you'd taken leave :
That you'd be gone, had I been ne'r fo certain,
We might have drank a Pot or two at parting ;
Or fry'd fome Bacon with an Egg ; or if
Into fome Steaks, we'd cut a pound of Beef,
And laugh'd a while, that had been fomething like ;
But to fteal off, was but a fneaking Trick.
My Landlady can tell, how I was troubled,
When I perceiv'd my felf fo plainly bubbled :

I ran like mad out at the Alley-Gate
To overtake you but it was too late:
When I confider'd I had loft my Coat,
If I had had a Knife I'd cut my Throat ;
Yet notwithftanding all the ills you did,
I Dream of you as foon as I'm in Bed ;
You tickle me, and cry, Do'ft like it *Saff*?
Oh wonderous well! and then methinks I laugh.
Sometimes we mingle Legs, and Arms, and Thighs;
Sometimes between the fheets, methinks does rife :
But when I wake and find my Dream's in vain,
I turn to fleep only to Dream again.
When I am up, I walk about my Garret
And talk I know not what----juft like a Parrot ;
I move about the Room from Bed to Chair,
And have no Satifactoin any where.
The laft time I remembēr you lay here,
We both were dry ith' Night, and went for Beer ;

Into

Into the Cellar by good luck we got,
What we did there, I'm sure you ha'n't forgot:
There stands, you know, an antiquated Tub,
'Gainst which, since that, I often stand and rub;
Only to see't, as much delight I take
As if the Vessel now were full of Sack;
But more to add unto my Discontent,
There's been no Drink ith' Celler since you went.
There's nothing but affords me Misery,
My Linet in the Cage, I fear will dye:
The Bird is just like me in every thing;
Like me it pines Like me it cannot Sing.
Now *Phaon*, pray take notice what I say,
If you don't bring the things you took away;
You know my Garret is four Stories high;
From thence I'll leap, and in the Streets I'll die:
May be you will refuse to come----Do--- do,
Y' had best let *Sapho* break her Neck for you.

> *Your afflicted Consort*, Sapho.

PHILLIS to DEMOPHOON:

The ARGUMENT.

Demophoon *was born in* Holland, *who took after his Father* Theseus, *pretending to the Art of Pyracy ; he was cast upon* Newcastle-Shore *by adverse Winds (as the Dutch Commentators say) but we are inform'd he came hither by his own choice. No sooner arriv'd, but he heard that one* Phillis, *a single Woman, kept an Inn in the Town ; There he took up his Quarters :* Phillis *observed him as a lusty Younker, and though his outward Habiliments were not very tempting ; yet his person perswaded her so far, that she Married him, and entrusted him with all. After some time, he told his Wife that his Occasions call'd him into* Holland *to see his Father, who he said, was a Man of mighty Substance ; He promised to Return within a Month, but hath not been heard of since. Therefore she writes to him this Letter ; but whether it came to his hands or no, hath been a question to this day.*

Y Our absence does discover your Disdain,

    You've done enough to make a stone complain;

                            You

You told me you wou'd ftay a Month,----no more;
But by my Nature I do find 'tis four.
I, who am Woman, and a Lover too,
Obferve the change of Moons,   much more than you:
Indifpofition in the Head, or Back,
Informs our Sex beyond an Almanack.
Sometimes I hop'd----but foon that Hope did fink;
Sometimes I thought----I knew not what to think.
I made my--felf a Liar———notwithftanding
There was no Ship---I fwore I faw you Landing.
Some Curfes on your Father I beftow,
That old *Dutch* Rogue, think I, won't let him go:
But then again, that cannot likely feem,
The Maggot bites----you're gone away from him ;
What if you fhould be wrack't when hither bound?
No,---you're to great a Villian to be down'd.
                                        (*Philly?*
Whom fhall I blame? whom but thy felf----fond
Who haft liv'd now Thirty years, and art fo filly.
                                        When

When first you did within my Doors set footing,
I fell in Love.---forsooth---A Pox of rutting;
The Devil sure will have that Doctor *Hymen,*
Who told me, that his business was to try---men:
He did believe---you'd prove an honest Man,
Marry'em said he, with all the speed you can;
The Good old Man his Substance to increase,
Would match a Helhound to a Saint for Fees:
You swore such dreadful Oaths as ne'r was heard,
By th' *Belgick* Lyon, and the Pirnce's Beard;
By *Opdam's* Ghost, and by the Dragon's Tail,
B' your Father's Head, and Mother's Farthingale;
By the great Cannons, and the Bloody Flag,
And by the *Hogan Mogans* of the *Hague*;
Your execrations put m' in such a fright,
That all the Hair about me stood upright:
If on your Head these Curses fall you've nam'd,
I must conclude, that certainly y'are damn'd;

Hearing

Hearing such bloody Oaths, you would not stay,

I made all haste I could to get y'away;

I furnished you with all I cou'd afford,

Bisket and Powder'd Beef I put aboard;

A Flask of Brandy to your girdle hung,

Better I'm sure, was never tipt o're Tongue:

And when I pach'd your Sails with antient Smock,
                                        (good luck;

I thought they wou'd have brought me home.

But stead of that----such was my Fatal Hap,

I prov'd the Instrument of your Escape:

When you came hither in a low Condition,

Did I not stuff your Gut with good Provision:

The Suit y' had on----was destitute of stitches,

I gave you then my Brother's Coat and Breeches;

But as for that---Pox on't--- I'll ne'r repent it,

What you had wanted, I had then presented;

If you had never paid---here's none would stop ye;

But I must be your Wife too ——like a Puppy:

I

I wiſh to God that very day we met,

That into Gaol I had been thrown for Debt;

Then if I'd ask'd the Queſtion ——you'd have ſaid

Thank you, forſooth, I'm not in haſte to Wed.

Well, well! Myn Hier! y've caught me now 'tis true,

I hope I am the laſt you will undoe.

The *Dutch* by Paint deſcribe each others Lives,

And draw their Neighbours Actions, and their (Wives:

They'l draw your Father as ſome petty Pirate,

Doing ſmall things, which People wont admire at.

He has been Rogue enough, but done no Wonders,

'Has rob'd a Fiſherman, of Eels and Flounders:

Perhaps he's Drawn making a Sailor drunk,

Diving in's Pockets——to equip his Punk;

Theſe are but Trifles to what you have done,

The Father's but a Coxcomb----to the Son:

You ſhall be Drawn, firſt in your tatter'd Cloaths,

Humbly complaining, full of Lies and Oaths;

And

And then you fhall be Rigg'd from head to foot,
And from your Mouth, this Label fhall come out ;
"Poor *Phillis*, of *Newcaftle* upon *Tyne* ——
"'Twas I that ruin'd---now you fee, I'm fine.
What muft I do ? I have not Trading here,
And all my Neighbours do but laugh and fleer ;
One cryes, Where is your Husband *Demo* ——foe ?
For your right Name, not one of 'em does know ;
Another cryes out---Hey ! for *Amfterdam* ;
What ! Was'a *Dutchman* Phillis---or a Sham ?
Thus (as they fay) they throw you in my Difh ;
Wou'd I cou'd have you here but with a wifh,
For thefe Rogues fake ; 'twould be good fport to fee
How well you wou'd belabour two or three ;
Then they'd change Tone, and cry---God blefs ye (both,
You are a handfom Couple, by my Troth :
No---'tis in vain to hope that you'l return,
I muft continue, as I am their fcorn ;

But

But yet I can't forget the parting Day,
I thought you wou'd have hugg'd your Breath away
At laft you fpoke---'twas this confounded Lye,
Phil, in a Month this o're again we'll try;
But I believe that trick you're trying now
With fome tun-belly'd *Rotterdam* ———*U'froe :*
If *Phillis* fhou'd be talk'd on by the *Dutch,*
You'l fay you never heard of any fuch.
Phillis ! Who's fhe ? Where does this *Phillis* dwell ?
If you don't know, *Demophoon,* I'll tell;
"This is *Newcaftle-Phillis,* fhe that did
"Once entertain you, Sir, at Board and Bed.
"Some fmall Remembrance *Phillis* hath deferv'd,
"Had not this *Phillis* been, you might have ftarv'd ;
"She gave you Money, like a foolifh Elf;
'At laft this *Phillis* gave away her---Self.
I am that *Phillis,* if I had my due,
That fhou'd have Hang'd my felf for Loving you:

It will not be too late to do it ftill,

And if I'm in a humour, 'faith I will.

Then on my Grave let thefe few lines be writ,

Which *Phillis* made her-felf in Moody fit.

> *Here* Phillis *lyes,*
> *Had fhe been wife,*
> *S'had Wed a Neighb'ring* Scotchman;
> *And then fhe might,*
> *Have liv'd in fpite*
> *Of any Drunken* Dutchman.

HYPERM-

HYPERMNESTRA to LINUS.

The ARGUMENT.

There was lately a Gang of English Highway-men, all of 'em having Wives or Whores in London. *Now the only means to detect 'em, was by bribing their Women. In order to which the Keeper of* Newgate *went to 'em all, promising them very fairly, and with all, using Arguments how serviceable they wou'd be to their Country, in Discovering them ; which they might easily do, when they came home to Bed. The Women were easily perswaded, And one Night, order'd the Keeper to be there at such a time, who seized them all ; but* Linus *was præadmonished by his Wife* Hypermnestra, *so he escaped away in her Cloaths ; She bore the brunt in his Apparrel, and was Taken (supposed to be a man) and Committed to* Newgate, *and put into Irons. The rest of the Thieves were Hang'd, her Tryal was respited, being not known who she was.* Hypermnestra *sends him this Letter.*

TO thee poor *Hypermnestra* now complains,

Such is the Torture of my Iron Chains :

Shall it be call'd in Law, a Crime so heinous,

For being ju┃t to my own Husband *Linus* ?

Let

Let 'em torment me on, I do not care,
I'll not tell who I am, nor where you are;
If they shou'd Hang me up instead of you,
To the last Gasp I swear I will be true:
I long to be reveng'd on tyofe curs'd Wives,
That did betray their Friends and Husbands Lives.
Such Men were not in *England* to be found,
They'd bid the Devil stand, on any ground;
And all the prizes that they got, they spent
Upon those Whores; yet they were not content,
Think on that Night we did together Sup,
When all the Company were Cock-a-hoop;
That fatal Night you all came from the Pad,
Your Booty very large, your hearts were glad;
Though in my sad Condition, 'tis not proper;
Yet, I can well remember all the Supper:
A stately Loin of Veal began the Feast,
I help'd you half the Kidney at the least;

C

Four

Four Turkey Poulets came next you wish'd they'd
(been
Four *Turkey* Merchants upon *Mile-End-Green*;

Roasted young Ducks, and Chickens fricazeed;

There was more meat than we cou'd eat indeed :

Wine in abundance---I drank none but 'Sack,

^But all you men did ply it with Pontack :

To th' top you fill'd a Glass, and drank to th' best---

The Health as you began it, seem'd a Jest ;

I took't in Earnest to my self, and knew

That I shou'd prove the best of Wives to you.

By Two a Clock you Men were almost Drunk,

Then each to bed went to his Spouse or Punk ;

If they were all as kind as you to me,

Never was such a Night of Lechery :

At last you sleep securely without warning

Of the strange Alterations in the Morning :

I knew betimes the Keepers wou'd be there,

And all the Night I sweat, 'tween Sport and Fear

At

At laſt I roſe, and 'bout the Room I walk'd,

And thus at Randum to my ſelf I talk'd ;

Have I not ſworn a Thouſand Oaths at leſt,

That I'd betray my Husband with the reſt ?

What muſt I do ? 'Tis true, I am his Wife ,

What ! muſt I damn my Soul to ſave his Life ?

Hang all the Oaths in Chriſtendom, ſaid I ;

He is my Husband, and he muſt not die.

With that I drew your Breeches on in haſt,

The Codpiece was ſo big, I was amaz'd ;

I walk'd into your Coat, hanging on Peg.

I loſt my head within your Perewig :

Having put on your Armour Cap-a-pee,

For by the weight, ſuch was your Cloaths to me ;

You reach'd your Arm acroſs----had I been there,

You would have had the other bout, I fear ;

I pull'd the Sheet and Blanket from the Bed,

I plainly then perceiv'd, 'twas as I ſaid :

Riſe

Rife *Linus*, Rife, faid I; be very quick;
This is no time for any wanton Trick;
You're all betray'd——The Confta ble's at Door,
You muft not ftay a minute of an hour.
I fhuffled on my Cloaths upon your back,
They did not fit—I heard my *Manteau* crack:
No fooner were you gone, but in they bounc'd;
They feiz'd on me, and fwore I fhou'd be trounc'd.
And here they have me faft with Bolt and Lock;
They know not yet that I have on a Smock.
Now you are fafe, and I am here, dear *Linus*
Let's ferioufly difcourfe th' Affair between us:
If all the truh to them I fhould difcover,
What can they fay? 'twas acted like a like Lover;
I may be fent to *Bridewel*, there they'l bang me;
But all the Law in *England* cannot hang me.
While I lye here—I am in little eafe,
But when all's told, what fhall I do for Fees?

If

If you don't ufe fome means to get me freed,

Within few days you'l hear that I am Dead;

And then 'tis like they'l bury me; if fo

Upon my Grave this Epitaph beftow:

Here lies a Wife, who rather than fhe'ld fail

To fave her Husband's Life, dy'd in a Jayl:

My Irons load me fo, I'm fit to cry,

I would write more, but cannot; fo God b'ye.

HYPERM-

HERMIONE to ORESTES:

The ARGUMENT.

Hermione *was the Daughter of* Menelaus *and* Hellen. *Her Mother ran away with a young Fellow, one* Paris, *they went together beyond the Seas. Her Husband who lov'd her well, perfu'd 'em, and after many years, found his Wife and refcu'd her from her Gallant, and without any refentment of the Injury, took her again. During their abfence, their Daughter (who had an Eftate left her by her Unkle) was committed to the Cuftody of her Grand-father, who marri'd her to a School-fellow and Cozen German of hers, by name* Oreftes. *Her Father brought home with him one* Pyrrhus *a wild young Fellow, to whom he Marri'd her again, taking no notice of the firft match. She filly harmlefs Girl, wonders at the defign, and to her Husband* Oreftes *writes this innocent Letter.*

TO thee I write my dear and only Cuz;

Nor will I be afraid to call thee Spoufe:

Though here's a Fellow come refolv'd to fwear

I am his Wife, and he will mak't appear;

He

He looks fometimes, as if he long'd to eat me,
Sometimes he looks fo gruff, as if he'd beat me:
He fays he is *Achilles* Son and Heir,
And bids me difobey him, if I dare ;
He kiffes me fo hard, the ftrongeft man,
He gets a top of me do what I can ;
With all my ftrength my Legs together joyn,
But with one Knee, hee'l open both of mine.
I call him Rogue and Rafcal, filthy Sot,
And all the beaftly Names I can get out:
I'm Marry'd Sirrah, therefore don't miftake it,
I have a Husband that will thwack your Jacket :
Yet that's all one, he cares not what is faid ;
But by the Hair he drags me into bed :
They talk of Girls, forc'd by unruly men,
They can't be forc'd fo much as I have been :
Yet all this while *Oreftes* comes not near me,
I am afraid you do not love your *Hermey* ;

You'l

You'l fight for Money, as you'd fight for Life,
And won't you fight a little for your Wife?
On while my Father mift my Mother *Hellen*,
Lord! There was fuch a noife, and fuch a yelling,
He rais'd up all the People in our Lane,
And ne'r was quiet, till fhe came again.
I wou'd not have you make a noife for me,
But come and kill this fellow quietly;
Give him a good found blow, and never fear man,
It is for me, your Wife and Cozin German.
You know my Guardian marri'd me to you
When we were both fo young, we could not do---
Now from beyond Sea comes my Father huffing,
And will needs marry me to this fame Ruffian,
He vapours here about his Country Blood,
I guefs your *Englifh* Familie's as good :
He fays, you've led a very wicked life,
And that you broke your Mothers heart with grief.

For

For talking fo of you, I'd flit his Tongue,
And pull his Eyes out too, if I were ftrong;
'Tis fomething ftrange, we're of a Generation
Where Ravifhing has been a mighty fafhion:
My Grandmother was ravifh'd by one *Swan*,
A little Couzin by another man;
My mother has been ravifh'd once or twice,
And I am ravifh'd now by her advice.
Muft I with fuch a Rogue as this be match'd?
A more unlucky Girle was never hatch'd.
My mother left me here a little Wench,
Juft big enough to clamber on a Bench;
She was ftark mad for that young fellow---*Paris*,
And after him fhe danc'd the new Fagaries
My Father for his life cou'd not forbear,
But ran a--catter-wawling after her;
Now they're come home, but with fuch alt'red
(looks,
As if they fome were ftrange Outlandifh fo'kes.

My

My Father has a Beard below his Band,

I did not know my Mother, fhe's fo tann'd:

Toward my good, what did fhe ever do?

When fhe was gone, I larn't to knit and fow;

I ufe my needle now as well's another,

But 'tis no God-a-mercy to my Mother.

When fhe came in, fhe knew not who I was;

This Girl, faid fhe, is grown a ftrapping Lafs,

She muft be marry'd or fhe'l grow too bufie;

                            (Huffy:

Look here, I have brought thee home a Husband,

With that he threw his Paws about my Neck;

Kill him, *Oreftes,* or my heart will break:

I draw the Curtains when he's faft afleep,

And out of Bed, foon as 'tis day, I leap;

But I do tofs and tumble all Night long,

As if by Bugs and Pifmires I'd been ftung:

Sometimes when I'm afleep, by chance there lies,

                            (thighs;

One of my hands fqueez'd clofe between his

I snatch't away as foon as e're I wake,
With as much fpeed, as if I'd felt a Snake ;
To th' other fide o'th' Bed, I jerk from him,
And fometimes lay one Breech upon the Beam ;
Then after me, he by degrees will fteal,
Pray Sir keep off, fay I, I am not well ;
He feems as if he did not underftand,
And then he reches out his hafty hand ;
I fpeak as plainly to him as I can,
I tell him I'm not fitting for a Man.
Pfhaw, Pfhaw ! fays he, I know you do but jeft.
'Pon the whole matter he's a filthy Beaft :
For God's fake *Orey*, Prethee-now contrive,
Some way or other that he may not live :
For here I take my Oath upon a Book,
If you don't get me off by hook or crook,
That we may do as marry'd People my,
I'll either kill my felf, or run away.

CANACE to MACAREUS:

Lately tranflated out of

O V I D

Now BURLESQU'D.

The ARGUMENT.

Macareus *and* Canace, *Son and Daughter of* Æolus *(a Trumpeter of the Guards) being from children brought up together, at the laſt grew ſo intimately acquainted, that they made bold to lie with one another.* Canace *prov'd with Child by her Brother* Macareus. *She was deliver'd in the houſe; and the Nurſe contriv'd to convey the Child through the Hall when* Æolus *was ſounding his Trumpet, accompany'd with ſeveral ſorts of Wind-muſick; notwithſtanding that noiſe, the ſhrill Cry of the Infant was over-heard by* Æolus, *who ſent it away to be left in the Streets, and expos'd to the mercy of the Pariſh; and to his Daughter* Canace *he ſent a*

Hal-

*Halter, with this Meſſage, ----This you have de-
ſerved, ----and you know how to uſe it.* Canace
hang'd her ſelf (*as you may gueſs*) *before ſhe wrote
this Letter.*

BEfore theſe rude, diſtracted **Lines** you read,
Believe the unlucky Authreſs of 'em **dead.**
Ever to ſee me more's beyond all **Hope,**
One hand a **Pen,** the other holds a **Rope** :
My bluſtring Father's troubled with a **Whim,**
And I muſt hang my ſelf to humour him.

But when he ſees my Carcaſe on the floor,
Surely he'll ceaſe to call me Bitch or **Whore** :
His puffing and his blowing will be in vain,
He cannot puffe me into life again :
His Mind is ſwell'd much bigger then his Face,
I am (he ſaies) his Family's **Diſgrace** :
All his great Friends and Kindred are provok't ;
What are his Friends to me when I am choak'd?

I

I wiſh that we had ſtifled one another
That night I clung ſo cloſely to you, Brother :
Why did you love me more then did become ye?
It had been happy, if y'ad kick'd me from ye :
When firſt, with pleaſure, I lay under you,
Would y'ad been lighter by a ſtone or two.

At firſt I wondred what ſhould be the matter,
I look'd like Death, and was as week as Water :
For ſeveral days I loath'd the fight of Meat,
And every night I chew'd the upper Sheet :
I'd ſuch Obſtructions, I was almoſt moap'd,
My Breath came ſhort, my —— were ſtop'd.

I call'd old Nurſe, and told her how it was ;
She, an experienc'd Bawd, ſoon groap'd the Cauſe :
Quoth ſhe, for this Diſeaſe, take what you can,
You'll ne'er be well, till you have taken Man :
When I was young, I thought I was bewitch'd,
I ſcrach't my Belly, for it alwaies itch'd.

The

The Truth I will no longer hide, said I,
I muſt enjoy my Brother, or I die :
She tickl'd me, and told me 'twas no Sin,
Nearer of Blood, ſaid ſhe, the deeper in :
Both you and I approv'd what Nurſe had ſaid,
So, without more a-do, we went to Bed :
You in my belly rummag'd all about,
To find this wonderfull diſtemper out :
Too ſoon 'twould be diſcovered, was my Fear,
I could have let you fearc'd for ever there :
But Nurſe can tell how I did ſigh and ſob
When we perceiv'd that you had done the Jobb.

 I made th' old Beldam foot it up and down
To every Quack and Mountebank in Town,
For *Dendelion*, and *Camelions-thighs*,
Spirit of Saffron mixt with *Vulters-eyes* :
I would have given all I had been worth,
'T' have kill'd the Child, before it had come forth :

But

But the ſtronge Rogue lay fencing in my Womb,
And did thoſe pois'naus Potions overcome:
Oh! when I ſaw the ninth Moon in the Wane,
Then I was in the Full----of grief and Pain;
        (thick;
Then, then my Throws came on m thick and
I groan'd but for my Life I durſt not ſchreik
Untill my Tortures came to ſuch a growth

         (Mouth:
That Nurſe with both her Hands did ſtop my
I ſhould have cry'd ſo loud, that every Neighbour
Would have diſcover'd I had been in Labour:
No woman yet that ever wore a Navel,
Endur'd ſo hard and ſo ſevere a Travel.

 I curs'd your Sex, and wiſh'd a Rot might come
On all the Stallions throughtout Chriſtendome.
At laſt you came; I knew you by your tread;
I peep'd at you, though I was almoſt dead:

        T'ward

(morse
T'ward me you seem'd to have some kind Re-
But look'd, as if you would have eaten Nurse.

   You held my back-parts, you could do no more;
Would you had never felt the Parts before.

   Sister, said you, you shall not die this bout,
We're both unluky, but, we'll rub it out.

   To see what words from those we love can do,
(Surely the Child within me heard you too,)
For streight he sprang forth from me, and did seem
To make his passage in a flowing Stream:
'Twas hard enough: but now's a harder Case,
To hide the Business from my Father's face;
We did consult how to devise a way
Thorough the Hall our Bastard to conveigh.

   My Father in Wind-musick still delighted,
And all the Gang that night he had envited:
Fellows that play on Bag-pipes, and the Fife;
The old man always lov'd a noiseful Life:

            D   They

They all did found together after Supper,
And then to carry 'em off, we thought, was proper.
   Nurfe, in her Apron took the little Brat,
Swath'd up in Linnin, Rufhes over that ;
Quite through the Hall fhe went her ufual pace,
And, unconcern'd her felf, humm'd *Chevy-Chafe*.
   Juft to the door s'had fafely carry'd him,
When the unlucky Wretch began to fcreme :
His little Organ made a fhriller noife
Than all the Fluits, Recorders, or Ho-boies :
The old man prick'd his ears up, like a Hare,
And after Nurfe ran nimbly, as the Air :
Whither fo faft, faid he, old Mother Trundle ?
Pray, let us fee, what have you in your Bundle :
Quoth Nurfe,—'Tis Miftrefs *Canny's* dirty Smoak,
Men into Womens fecerts fhould not look.
   He puff'd away the Rufhes from her Lap,
And there appear'd the little fprauling Ape :

                        'Zound's

'Zounds, faies my Father, What is here ? A Kid !
My Daughter *Canny*'s finely brought to bed ?

He rais'd fo great a Tempeft in the Houfe,
I thought that Hell it felf was broken loofe ;
He rag'd fo loud, the Bed fhook under me;
Methought I was in fome great Storm at Sea :
He rufh'd into the Room, and did difcover
The bloody Symptoms of a Child-bed Lover :
Our Sexes Stains by him were here difcry'd
                                        (hide :
Which Women from their own dear Husbands
With his own hands he did defign to wound me,
But that he faw fomething like Murther round me;
The Baftard in the Streets he did expofe,
And what will be his deftiny, God knows :
The little Knave, with Tears, did feem to anfwer;
As who fhould fay, I beg your pardon Granfir,
Out went old *Trump* ; I by his Looks could find
There was fome mifchief hatching in his mind,

In came a Fellow of the *Bag-pipe* Gang
Whofe very Whiskers feem'd to fay, go hang ;
Before his words came out his tongue did falter ;
At laft he fpake, *Canny,* look here's a Halter :
Your Father faies, 'Tis this you do deferve ;
If you'll not ufe it, you may live and ftarve.
His moft obedient Daughter he fhall think me :
If I don't hang my felf, the Devil-fink me.

   Since Whoreing does produce fuch ftrange effects
Would I'd been born a Monfter without Sex :
Let my young Sifters all be warn'd by me,
And curb betimes Inceftuous Lechery.

   This I requeft of you, Dear Brother *Mac.*
That of our wretched Child fome care you'd take ;
If you can find him out, be not unwilling,
Towards his maintenance, to drop a fhilling.

   Let thefe my laft words be obferv'd by you,
As I obey my Father's : —— fo, — Adieu.

A R I-

ARIADNE to *THESEUS*,

Lately tranſlated out of

O V I D

Now BURLESQU'D.

The ARGUMENT.

Theſeus, *an Engliſh Gentleman, and one who for his diverſion admir'd Travelling, eſpecially on Foot, having ſafely arriv'd at* Calais, *walk'd oneaſily from thence to* Paris, *where he had not long been but he receiv'd an unmannerly Juſtle from a Cavalier of* France : Theſeus, *whoſe great Soul could not brook the leaſt Affront, reſented this ſo highly, that he challeng'd him, fought him, and after a long and skilful Diſpute between 'em, fairly kill'd him :* Theſeus *was impriſon'd in the* Baſtile ; *During his Reſtraint he held a League with* Ariadne, *the Keeper's daughter : And, though the Priſon was as difficult as a Labyrinth, (ſuch is the power of* Love,)*

D 3

ſhe

she soon contriv'd a way for his Escape by night: and he, accompany'd with Mistress Ariadne, footed it back to Calais; where, both lodging together at the Red-Hart, he very unkindly took the advantage of her Snoaring, and stole from her early in the morning; and went off with the Pacquet-boat to Dover; from whence he genly walk'd to London: Ariadne sends him These.

NO savage *Bear*, no *Lyon*, *Wolf*, or *Tyger*,
      (*Rigor*;
Would ever use his Mistress with such

D'ye think you don't deserve ten thousand Curses,

For leaving me in Pawn at Monsieur *Forces*?

I wonder what the Tavern-people think!

For here I sit, and dare not call for Drink.

While by your side I innocently lay,

You might have taken leave, a civil way:

I was half waken'd from a pleasant Sleep

By th' melancholly sound of *Chimney-sweep*:

I stretch'd my Leg, to find out my Bed-fellow,

But I could groap out nothing but the Pillow:

       Thinking

Thinking t' have hugg'd you in my Arms fo clofe
One of the Bed-ftaffs almoft broke my Nofe:
Thef. Thef. faid I, I hope you are not gone:
I might as well have call'd the Man i'th' Moon:
I rent my Head-cloaths off, *mortdieu! mordieu!*
What will become of me? What fhall I do?
I op'd the Cafement as the Morning dawn'd;
And could plainly fee that I was pawn'd,
With calling you I tore my Throat to pieces,
The Eccho jeer'd me with the name of *Thefeus*:
To th' top of all the houfe I ran undreft;
The people thought that I had been poffefs'd:
At laft, I fpy'd you in the Pacquet-boat;
I knew it was you or fo at leaft I thought:
Had you been walking, I had known your Stride,
And guefs'd your Strutt from all Mankind's befide:
Both Seas and Winds muft needs be kind to thee
Thou art fo like 'em in Inconftancy.

D 4   I thump

I thump my Breaſt, I rage, I ſtorm and fume;
The Houſe deſires I would diſcharge my Room:
Quoth one o'th' Servants, Miſtreſs *Ariadne's*
Paſt all recovery, overwhelm'd with Madneſs:
Another crys, *Mam'ſell Com' portez vou'* ?
Fetch me my *Theſ.* ſaid I, What's that to you.
When in the Boat I cou'd no longer ſee you,
Ten thouſand De'ills of Hell, ſaid I, go we' you.
        (Wine ;
 They think I'm drunk, I'm ſure'tis not with
The Score's too large; and you have left no Coin.
Into a Corner I am ſometimes dogg'd,
And there I cry as if I had been flogg'd:
Sometimes I roul my Self upon the Bed,
And act thoſe poſtures o're that once we did:
To my own ſelf with pleaſure I repeat,
Here lay my Head, and there I put my Feet!
I often call to mind our amorous Work;
Then here, methinks I have you with a Jerk.

Sometime they talk, that Ships are safe at home :
I listen then, to hear if you are come.

   Were I a Man, into the Seas I'd douse,
And after you I'd swim, and bilk the house :
If I should offer to run home again,
My Father'd keep me in an Iron-chain ;
I have betray'd the old Man's Trust for you ;
I may go whistle for a Portion now :
When, for your sake, I stole the Prison Keys,
I little thought to see such days as these :
Oh ! when your L O V E was mounted to a pitch,
You hugg'd me as the Devil hugg'd the Witch ;
You swore, with Oaths most desperate and bloody,
The Queen of *France* to me was but a Dowdy.
I have more Whymses then a dancing *Bear*,
Sometimes I dream the Constable is here :
And though the Waiters very often wheedle,
Yet I suspect that they will bring the Beadle.

                 Again,

Again, I fear they'll fpirit me away,
And fend me Slave into *Virginia* :
I was not bred a Drudge from the beginning,
Except it were to wafh my Fathers Linnen.

    Either to Sea or Land I durft not look,
To Heav'n I can't ; you've ftole my Prayer-book :
Your Valour made my Fortune fo untoward,
I would to God that you had been a Coward :
Diftreffed *Ariadne* now complains,
Becaufe fuch fprightly blood runs in her Veins ;
They fay we *French* are very Hot, 'tis true;
But yet our Sparks are Froft and Snow to you :
Curft be the time when you firft learnt to fence,
(Though that does never alter Men of fence.)

    I fancie in what pofture you were found,
One Foot heav'd up, the other on the Ground :
As much of Warlike Grace you did difcover
As any *Roman* Statue in the *Loure*.

Methinks

Methinks I hear you fpeak to th' Cavilier,

Sa ! *Sa* ! *Monfieur*, I have you here and there :

But now your valiant Acts are loft for ever,

By fneaking off, like a *French-Ribbon-Weaver*.

   Had I not drank that *Brandy* over night,

I cou'd have wak'd, and fo have ftop'd your Flight.

Curft be the Wind which was fo kind to you ;

Curft be the Boat, and curft be all its Crew ;

Curft may I be for trufting what you faid ;

Curft may all Lovers be that Snore in Bed.

Poor *Ariadne*, thou art finely ferv'd,

Thy too much Love has brought the to be ftarv'd:

The Servants pitty me, and fay't's a hard cafe,

I've nothing here to pay 'em with but Carcafe :

This Carcafe too has wept out all its Juice,

'Tis grown fo dry, 'tis fit for no Man's ufe.

Think, when you're rev'ling in your Cups at *London*,

That your Poor *Ariadne* here, is undone,

And

And when you come where people do refort,
To hear your Travels told were pritty fport :
With what tough bit of Flefh you did engage;
You thought you fhould be killing him an Age :
Do not forget me when you tell your Tale,
Tell'em how I releas'd y'out of Goal ;
And how with you I ftole on foot through Allys ;
And, pray forget not, that I am pawn'd at *Callais*:
And, when this Tale to your Companion's told,
Imagine *Ariadne* ftiff and cold :
When dead, they'll bury me in fome back Garden,
For I can't give the Parifh-Clerk a farthing.

   And 'tis for you I all thofe Sorrows prove;
So, Mr. *Thefeus*, thank you for your Love.

LEANDER

LEANDER to HERO:

The ARGUMENT.

Leander *an Uſher of a School, and chief Poet of* Richmond, *having contracted a more then ordinary Acquaintance with Miſtreſs* Hero *of* Twitnam, *a Governeſs or Tutreſs to young Ladies ; ſuch a reverential eſteem had they procur'd to themſelves at each place, that they could not conveniently meet without great ſcandal ; therefore the Uſher frequently ſwam over to his Miſtreſs by night, but at this time the* Thames *was ſo rough, that he was conſtrained to convey his mind to* Hero *by a Waterman in theſe Poetical Lines, wherein Love and Learning ſtrive to outvie each other.*

YOur faithful Lover ſends this Bille' dou'x.

Stuff'd full of Love, but not a word of news.

Believe not, I think much of any Labour,

Cou'd I have come my ſelf, I'd ne're ſent Paper ;

The *Thames* is rough, the Winds ſo hard do blow,

I ſcarcely got a Waterman to go.

And

And if I wou'd have given a thouſand pound,

This was the only Fellow to be found.]

I ſtood upon the Shoar, while he went off,

The Boat once gone, I thought 'twas well enough.

I muſt be careful whom I ſend by Water,

Our Family begins to ſmoak the matter:

Juſt as the Letter went, I had a fancy

Came in my head, I cou'd have made a Stanza :

Go Paper, go, and kiſs a whiter hand,

That oft hath put *Leander* to a ſtand.

Methinks, the Nymph perfumes it with her Breath,

And bites the wax of with her Ivory Teeth :

Her Sheperd would be glad to be ſo bit,

Untill th' aforeſaid Teeth together met.

But then think I, theſe whymſes ſhee'll condemn

The hand that writes, ſhould rather make me ſwim,

Bold ſtrokes in Poetry ſhe hardly blames,

But ſuch bold ſtroaks ſhou'd be upon the Thames :

Methinks

Methinks it is an Age fince I fwam o're,

I long untill each Arm, does prove an Oar.

Fully refolv'd I came to'th water fide,

And thought the fpace between us but a ftride.

I faw your houfe, and wifh'd that I cou'd clamber

To your watch--- light in the fupremeft Chamber:

I pull'd off Coat and doublet twice or thrice,

But then I thought,---- be merry and be wife.

Thus I in Verfe fpake to the mighty *Boreas*,

(rious;

Thou bluftring youth—— pray tell me why fo fu-

Tho' amongft Winds thou art a great Commander,

Blow gently for the fake of poor *Leander*.

I crofs no Sea (Here *Thames* is call'd the Sea,

Becaufe it doth with lofty Verfe agree.)

I crofs no Sea to *Afia* or to *Afrique*,

Upon the Account of Sublunary Traffique:

Ingots of Gold! alas! I do not feek 'em,

Give me my Heroes Love, then *omnia mecum*.

Boreas

Boreas himself does sometimes leave off roaring
And goes a---woing, I'll not say a---whoring.
For several uses you, your breath may spare,
Do not so fiercely move our *Richmond* Air.
But all was vain, *Boreas* was still unkind,
I did repeat my Verses to the wind.
Had I but wings, I'd soar above the People
And place my self just now on *Twitnam* Steeple.
I well remember that first night I swam,
That happy night I first to *Twitnam* came;
I put of all my cloaths, with them my fears,
And dous'd into the *Thames* o're head and ears.
The Moon took---care *Leander* should not sink,
And stole before me like a lighted Link:
I thank'd her for her Love, and thus did greet her,
As far as my poor Talent went---in meeter.
Ah gentle Moon, because thou'rt kind to me,
I wish *Endymion* may be so to thee:

And

And as with him thou hold'st a private League
With thy broad Eye, so wink at my Intrigue.
Under correction to your Heavenly sence,
Your case and mine have little difference.
A Goddess you love one of human Birth,
My Mistress is a Goddess upon Earth :
Such sort of Beauty as she wears, is given
Only to such as do belong to Heaven.
And if you are not of the self same mind,
Begging your Pardon, *Cynthia*, you're blind.
With such like words I got near *Twitnam* sands,
And nothing all the way saw I but Swans.
At last I spy'd your Candle on the top,
Aye! now all's well, thought I, there is some hope.
But when you put your head out from the Caze- ment,
Then was *Leander* struck into amazement ;
For two Lights more did from the Window seem,
Which made the artificial one look dim.

E

Your

Your Eyes the Moon, and Candle made juft four ;
I, like fome Prince was lighted to the fhoar.
But you're to blame, when you perceiv'd me come,
Nurfe fayes, fhe cou'd not keep you in the room,
But in your fhift you wou'd be running down ;
You'l get fome violent cold, and then you're gone.
But to fay truth, thou art a loving Tit,
Thou hug'ft me in thy arms all dripping wet :
I can but think how ftraingly I did look,
When you put o're my head a Holland Smock ;
And hand in hand thus walking from the *Thames*,
We feem'd the Ghofts of two diftreffed Dames.
But when we came to Bed, we underftood,
We were no Ghofts, but real Flefh and Blood :
We did repeat more pleafures in one hour,
Than fome dull Lovers do in forty fcore ;
Becaufe we knew our time was very fhort,
We cou'd not tell the number of our fport.

Aurora

Aurera does from *Tithon*'s Bed escape,
Tithon perhaps will take the other nap,
See her Postillian *Lucifer* before,
And now the Bus'nefs of the Night is o're;
The day appears, *Leander* muft be jogging,
And home agen among the Boyes a-flogging.
My well beloved *Amo* I forfake,
And to dull *Doceo* now I muft go back.
And Subftantive I'll always be to thee,
My pritty Verb *Deponent* thou fhalt be.
If we were in conjuction day and night,
Leander would not prove a heteroclite:
In Grammer we make Noun to joyn with Noun,
Why fhou'd not *Twitnam* joyn with *Richmond,*
(Town?
'Twou'd make one mad to think a foolifh River,
Or any furly Winds fhould Lovers fever:
But hold *Leander*, let no Seas nor Wind
Difturb the quiet Freehold of thy Mind.

When

When firſt I croſt--my thought the Fiſh did gaze,

The Salmon ſeem'd to peep upon my Face;

I could hear Boatmen call from Weſtern Barge,

What Fiſh is that, my thinks 'tis very large,

They'd call me Porpus, and they'd jeer and flout me;

But now by th' name of Brother they ſalute me:

How d'ee ſays one; Good morrow t'other cryes;

I civilly return them, *Bona dies.*

The Fiſhermen that bobs all night for Eel,

Now ſayes, Your Servant, Sir, I wiſh you well:

God ſend you ſafe on t'other ſide the Water,

I ſay unto him, *Salvus ſis piſcator.*

I hope thoſe Halcyon Nights will ſoon return;

For want of 'em, does poor *Leander* mourn.

Eut if ſuch ſtorms in Summer time does hinder,

How ſhall I e're get to the in the Winter?

If I do venture in, and ſhould be drown'd,

I hope by thee my Body will be found.

Thou'lt

Thoul't roul it up in Holland or in Bucram,

Then may I truly fay---*mors mihi Lucrum.*

But let not this poffefs you I am dead,

A foolifh whimfey came into my head,

We fhall have many pleafant Nights between us,

I'll come and hugg my *Hero ore-tenus.*

Pray put thefe Lines up fafe, for fear you loofe 'em,

In that warm place where I would be, your Bofom:

And in a little time, difpute it not,

I'll come and juftifie what I have wrot:

For when the wheather changes I'll not fail ye,

And untill then thou ---- *dulce decus Vale.*

HERO's *Answer*.

Leander, thank you kindly for your Letter,
Though if y'ad come your self it had been
(better;
I cannot reft, I know not what's the matter,
I'm all afire, to have you crofs the Water.
We Women when we've any thing to do,
Are ten times more defirous of't than you;
Having difmift your little Boyes from School,
You can walk out i'th' the Evening when 'tis cool;
You can divert your felf a hundred wayes,
I only ftand upon the fhoar and gaze:
You have a Green in which you bowl or bett,
And now and then three or four fhillings get;
Or to the Tavern, when you pleafe you go
And drink a Bottle with a Friend or fo;

While

While I fit moap'd---like a neglected Cat,
And now and then with old dry Nurfe I chat:
What's your opinion, Nurfe, and tell me truly,
D'ye think the Wind to Night will be unruly?
What will *Leander* come? or keep away?
'Faith I don't know, fayes fhe, 'tis like he may;
Such droufie anfwers I do feldom mifs,
D'ye think I han't a bleffed time of this?
Up to my Chamber, when 'tis Night, I get,
And in the Window is my Candle fet;
Perhaps I read a Play, or fome Romances,
I foon grow weary of fuch Idles Fancies:
Then I perufe your Letter o're again,
And more and more admire your learned ftrain;
Then I ask Nurfes Judgment in the cafe,
But fhe old Soul's, as dull as e're fhe was;
I make her ftand uprigh (there I miftake,
She can't ftand fo---for fh' as a huckle back)

I mean, I fet her fomewhere in the Room,
And fhe's to act as if you juft were come;
My only Joy (fay I) thou'rt welcome hither,
How didft thou fwim to me this ftormy wheather?
Speak, let me hear fome Mufick from thy mouth,
Nurfe nods, and fays---I'm pritty well forfooth:
Thus I beguile the time till Morning----peep,
Then I go into Bed and fall afleep.
And there I do enjoy you in my dreams,
Spite of the Devil or the rougher Thames.
Methought I faw you come ftark naked in,
Wet were your locks, and dropping was your Skin
I with an Apron rub'd you up and down,
And dry'd you from the toe unto the crown;
Then prefently we hugg'd with fuch a force,
I fhook the Bed, and wak'd and ftartled Nurfe;
And finding it to be a Dream---no more,
I grew as melancholy as before.

If

f in a dream fuch tickling Joyes appear,

Much pleafanter 'twou'd be, if you were here;

don't know what to think : you us'd to fay,

Ten Thoufand Devils fhould not ftop your way:

Why fhould the danger at this time be more?

The Wind blows hard, and fo it did before;

But now I fee which way 'tis like to drive,

A *Richmond* Wench as fure as I'm alive;

Ah! fay ye fo? why then it is for her

This Storm is rais'd, *Leander* cannot ftir.

But hang't that cannot be, I'm turn'd a fool,

Leander was and is an honeft Soul:

As foon as I had faid thefe words of you,

The Candle burn't not as it us'd to do;

Sayes Nurfe, there is a ftranger in the Light,

Mafter *Leander* will be here to Night;

With that fhe took the Brandy bottle up,

And pull'd from thence a very hearty fup,

Sayes

Sayes fhe---if what I fay fhould prove untrue,
I wifh this bleffed draught may ne're go through;
Therefore let's fee you hear to night dear *Nandy*,
Or elfe poor Nurfe muft never more drink Brandy.
Perhaps you fancy you take double pains,
And make to great a trefpafs on your Reins,
To fwim fo far as you have us'd to do,
And after that to pleafe a Miftrefs too;
Half of one half I'd eafe you if I cou'd,
And meet you in the middle of the flood;
But from the latter fervice never flinch,
I fhould be loath to bait you half an inch;
But after all excufing what I'ave faid,
Pray do not crofs the River hand o're head;
I dream't laft night, I hope 'tis no ill Luck,
A Spaniel Dog was hunting of a Duck,
There were fome reads which under Water grew,
And more, perhaps, than the poor Spaniel knew.

He

e was entangled there, and there was found,
came to help him, but the Curr was drown'd.
do not tell this dream to make you tardy,
ut as a Caution not to be fool-hardy.
he Wind will soon be laid, the *Thames* be clear,
hen you may cross it, without wit or fear :
Make much of this, for if you fail me, then
By all the Gods I'll never write agen.

LAODAMIA

LAODAMIA to PROTESILAUS,

Lately Translated out of

O V I D:

Now BURLESQU'D.

The ARGUMENT.

In the War between England *and* Holland, *one* Protesilaus, *an* English *Lieutenant of a Fifth Rate Frigat, being Wind-bound upon the* Downs ; *his Wife* Laodamia, *hearing he was not gone off, sent him this Letter ; and, like a fond Wife, gives him strict Caution to avoid Fighting.*

A Health to your Prosperity goes round,
    And to your safe return before you're
                      (drown'd :
My Neigybour *Jackson's* Wife began it to me ;
If I don't wish it, may it ne'er go through me :

                    We

We drink, and fancie to our felves in vain,

That the good Winds will blow him back again.

I hate the noife of a tumultuous Sea,

Give me a Tempeft rais'd by you and me ;

A Storm in which all Parts about us fhake,

When we can hear the Bed beneath us crack.

At *Gravefend,* when we took our laft Adieu,

The Parting Kifs, remember, I gave you :

I, like a fhitten Girle, began to cry ;

I had no mind, methoughts, to fay, God b'w'y :

I heard Tarpaulins roar out, Hoife up Sail ;

On Board, on Board ; here comes a merry Gale :

In fuch brisk Gales poor Women don't delight,

They blow away the pleafures of the night :

As you went off, I could not bear the Lofs,

A Qualm came o'er my Stomach quite-a-crofs :

Old Mother *Crump,* a very fubtile *Croan,*

Saw by my Looks that I was almoft gone :

A Pint

A Pint of Brandy prefently fhe brought,
And made me drink a very hearty draught ;
She fhew'd her Love, but what great good has't
(done?
How can I live with comfort now you're gone?
I wake, and find no Husband by my fide ;
I often think 'twere better I had dy'd :
Till you return, I'll ne'er be dreft agen ;
I have not comb'd my head the Lord knows when
A Glafs of Wine fometimes my heart does cherifh
Wer't not for that, I fanfie I fhou'd perifh :
Becaufe I go fo taudry, like a Punk,
Some, that don't know me, think that I am drunk :
My Neighbours often tell me, Miftrefs *Protef----,*
You go fo ftrangely, all the Street takes notice !
Says one, You do your Husband's Friends difgrace ;
For fhame ! Put on a Peticoat with Lace :
Why fhould they think that I would wear a lac'd-
(coat ?
When my poor Husband's in a Seaman's waftcoat?

Should

Should I adorn my Head with curles and Towers?

When a poor Skippers Cap does cover yours.

   The Plaguy *Dutch* ; that they fhould break the
                           (Peace,

And not fubmit to us in *Englifh* Seas :

Though, for my own particular, I fwear,

If I could once again but have you here,

Let *Dutch* have Liberty to fifh and foul,

I would not care a Farthing, by my Soul.

Methinks I fee you now, and, by your looks,

You are engaging with a Butter-box :

Methinks juft now a Bullet did efcape,

And hit my Neck, juft in the very Nape.

  But oh ! I fween, when I do think of *Trump* !

His Ships now giving yours a bloody Thump !

Blefs us, faid I, Now, you are difpatch'd !

That Dog has been at Sea 'fore you were hatch'd :

For Heaven's fake avoid him if you can,

He's certainly the Devil of a Man !

If any Ship does make up towards you,

You may fay fure *Van-Trump*'s among the Crew :

There's not a Shot does to your Veffel come,

But I receive the Pain on't here at home.

What am I better if you beat the *Dutch*,

And you come hither hopping on a Crutch ?

How finely 'mong the Neighbourhood 'twou'd
(fhow,

To fee you ftrut upon a timber Toe ?

To rout the Foe is fome great Adm'ral's Office,

In thefe Engagements you are but a Novice :

Your fingle Valours nothing on the Sea,

Your Combate fhould be hand to hand with me.

Would I were in the Fleet with *Trump or Ruyter,*

To them I would become an Humble Suitor,

And point out to them where your Squadron lay,

Directing them to fhoot another way :

I'd fpeak t'em thus ; Great Souls of *Amfterdam*
,

Pray hear a filly Woman, as I am ;

And

And let your Cannon my poor Husband fhun,
He knows not to difcharge a little Gun:
If you were Women, as you're Warelike Men,
He would perform great Actions wi' you then:
Your Fighting, Skirmifhing, and Breaking Bones,
Are only fit for Men that want their Stones.

Juft as you were commanded to your Ship,
Remember, at the Stairs your Foot did flip;
Think on that Slip, and, when the *Dutch* are fhoot
(ing
Duck down your Head, as if you wanted footing;
I wifh your Captain fome good Coward were,
And durft not bring the Veffel up for fear:
I wifh to God he would not fail too faft;
You'l come too foon, although you come the laft.
When you return, they'll ask how matters ftand;
I hope you'll know no more than we at Land.

All the day long I fmell no fent but Powder,
Each minute Guns go louder off and louder.

F   Moft

Moft marry'd women long till it be night,

But, for my part, I hate the thoughts of it;

Unlefs, by chance, I fleep, and dream of you:

Fancy's the kinder Husband then o'th' two:

And when I wake and feel the Linnen wet,

I find, I've wept for joy upon the Sheet:

This to Enjoyment gives but half content;

When fhall we meet together by confent?

Oh, how I long to hear you tell in Bed

Some ftrange Romantick Tale of what you did!

But when you find you can't prolong the Jeft,

And, being at *Stand*,---kifs out the reft.

    Againft both Wind and Tide why will you go?

You'd fcarce come home if Wind and tide faid no.

You fight, methinks, about fo mean a thing,

Which fhould have Privilege of catching *Ling*:

Old-Ling I hate worfe than a Common Whore;

(Would you lov'd Fighting with the *Dutch* no

I ate it once, and that againſt my will,
And ſometimes fancy that I ſmell on't ſtill.
But though thou art expos'd to Seas and **Wind,**
It is ſome caſe unto my troubled **Mind**
To ſee thy comely Picture in the Hall,
Drawn to the Life with Charcoal on the Wall:
I prattle to it as if thou wert here;
'Tis late; Pr'ythee let's go to Bed, my Dear:
Methinks thou ſay'ſt; I'll humour thee for once;
Thou'lt work me at the laſt to Skin and Bones:
I kiſs the Wall and do my Ceeks beſmear,
And ope my Mouth, as if your Tongue was there.
By all the pleaſant Poſtures of Delight,
By all the Twines and Circles of the Night,
By the firſt minute of our Nuptial Joys,
When you put fairly for a Brace of Boys,

I do

I do conjure you, have a fpecial care,

And let not faucy Danger come to near;

For when I hear that thou art knock'd o'th' head,

I'll hold you ten to one that I am dead,

O E N O N E

OENONE to PARIS.

The ARGUMENT.

Paris *was the Son of* Priam *a Wealthy Old Citazen and Alderman of* London. *When* Hecuba *his Mother was big with Child of him, she dream't 'a foolish conceited Dream, which occasion'd Old* Priam *to consult* Lilly, *who told him, That* Paris *in process of time would occasion his house to be burnt down. Therefore the credulous Alderman sends him into the Country far* North *to be dispos'd of as a By-blow. When he grew fit for Service he was entertain'd in a Gentleman's House, where he contracted a Bosom-acquaintance with* Oenone *a Young Wench and fellow Servant with him in the same house. His Father began to come to himself, and hearing where he was, sent for him, and own'd him as his Son; but before that, he had disengaged himself from Service, and ran away with one* Hellen, *who was VVife to* Menelaus. Oenone *being inform'd of All these proceedings, writes to him this Letter.*

A Fter my hearty Love to you remembr'd.

Hoping you are not in Body distemper'd,

More

More than my felf at the writing hereof;
If it be fo, we are both well enough :
Your Ufage has been fuch to poor Oenone,
That none but fuch a fool as I would own'e'e ;
I hear you're run away with Menels Wife,
I pitty her, fhe'll lead a bleffed Life ;
What mighty mifchief have I done, I wonder ;
You'l never have a younger, nor a founder.
If by my means y'had met with fome difafter,
Had I procur'd you Anger from your Mafter ;
If I had giv'n you that they call a Clap,
You'd had fome fmall Excufe for your Efcape :
But now you've had your ends, away to fneak,
Come ! come ! thefe things would make a body,
                    (fpeak.
You were not then fo Uppifh----when you faid,
A Dutchefs was a T —— t' a Servant Maid ;
You were a Groom your felf, you know 'tis truth
Not all your Greatnefs now — can ftop my mouth;

                                If

If you were able to keep houſe you ſwore
You'd marry me for all I was your Whore.
We were together on a Summers day,
Both in the Stable, on a Truſs of Hay ;
You can't forget ſome pretty paſtimes there,
No body ſaw us but the Cheſnut Mare :
You ſaid ſuch glorious things the very Beaſt
Prick'd up her Ears, and thought you were in Jeſt;
But I did prove th' verrier beſt o'th' two,
For like an Aſs I thought that all was true ;
Soon after----you were taken from the Stable,
To wait upon your Maſter at his Table ;
To undertake it you ſeem'd very loath,
Did I not teach you then to lay a Cloath ?
There's no man but muſt have his firſt beginning,
Who learnt you then to fold your Table Linnen ?
Did you not often when the Cloath were ſpread,
Juſt in the middle put your Salt and Bread ?

F 4

You

You have been threatned oft to lofe your place,

Becaufe you knew not how to fill a Glafs;

You pour'd in Wine up to the very top,

I told you you fhould fill but to the knob.

Did I not fhew you how to broach your Drink,

And tilt the Veffel when't begin to fink ?

I was your deareft Honey----all that while

There was not fuch a Girle in Forty mile :

You carv'd my name upon the Trencher-Plates,

And on the Elms before the outward Gates ;

And as we fee in time thofe Elms encreafe,

So will my name grow greater with the Trees ;

And any one that ftands but at the door,

May fee *Oenone* (your obedient Whore.)

You never have been well, fince thofe three Maids,

Rather thofe impudent and bold-fac'd Jades

Differ'd among them----felves, which it fhould be,

That had the cleanlieft fhap of all the Three.

To

To you they came when you were in the Clofe,
The Little Field that was behind the Houfe,
Stark naked did they come from top to toe,
Paris, fay they, we will be Judg'd by you.
Heavens preferve you Eye-fight---how you gaz'd,
Nor could you fpeak a word, you were fo maz'd ;
At laft you Judg'd with many a hum ! and haw !
Venus the fineft Wench that e're you faw.
This was a *Whitfon* Frolique, as they faid,
A pretty prank to fhew you all they had.
To fee how naked Women are bewitching,
Since that y'have minded nothing elfe but bitching.
Soon after that your project was of ftealing
That over-ridden Whore that Miftrefs *Hellen* :
I muft be gone a little while, you faid,
(Then was this Bus'nefs brooding in your head.)
You kift me hard as if I cou'd not feel,
And fwore that you wou'd be as true as fteal :

Said

Said you----Doubt nothing, for the case is plain,
I'm proved the Son of an Old Alderman,
And sent for home my Father's very ill,
I must be by, at making of his will;
Oh that we cou'd but bury the old Cuff,
Then marry you, all wou'd be well enough.
You may've a richer Wife, but not a better,
For I am no such despicable Creature:
Not to disparage your good Lady Mother,
I can behave my self as well's another.
No Wife like me was there in Christendom,
When you were honest *Pall*—Squires *Sheepeard's*
(Groom.
My Father's but a plain Old Man, 'tis true,
But's Daughter ha's been bred up as high as you.
He is an honest Man, what e'r I am,
And may be sav'd as soon as Master *Priam*.
Were I your Wife, my carriage shou'd not shame
Your Mother *Hec.*----tho' shee's a stately Dame.

What though thefe hands have us'd a Drippin-pan,

Yet on occafion they can furle a Fan.

Now on a little Folding Bed I lye,

(Tho' in that Bed fometimes lay you and I)

Yet I know how perhaps to hold my head,

If I were carried to a Damafque Bed.

If you had marry'd me y'had met with quiet,

What can y' expect from her but noife and riot ?

You now have caught a moft notorious Strumpet ;

Befides 'tis known, as if y'ad blown a Trumpet ;

Where e're you come you'l meet with frumps and
(Jeers,

Her Husband too, will be about your Ears.

In little time from you fhe will be budging,

She'l lye with any body for a Lodging.

When firft of all we clofely were acquainted,

(Which now it is too late, I have repented)

Caffandra was a Gipfey in the Town,

Who went a Fortune-telling up and down ;

I gave

I gave her broken meat, which we cou'd fpare,
Shee'd tell me all my Fortune to a hair :
You love (fayes fhe) a Man not tall nor fquat,
But a good hanfome Fellow, (mark ye that ?)
This youth and you 'tis likely may do well,
If he efcape but one----they call her *Nell.*
But if they two fhould chance to lye together,
Hee'll break the heart of you, and of his Father.
Who this *Nell* was, I cou'd not chufe but wonder ;
But now I know who 'tis---a Pox confound her !
I'll make *Caffandra* 'Liar tho', in part ;
You've vex'd me, but you ne're fhall break my
(heart.
This very Whore I fpaek on, ran-away
With fuch another Fellow t'other day,
And when her cloaths were gone, and money la-
(vifh'd,
She came and told her Husband fhe was ravifh'd.
I'm fure I'm true, for here fince you were gone,
Hath been fome loving Boobyes of the Town,

One

One of the Fellows furely is a Satyr,

He follows me, and fwears he'll watch my water:

We have a Servant come----pretends to Phyfick,

He hath a Cure for any one that-is-fick;

He cures the Tooth-ach; if your Finger's cut,

A Plaifter to it prefently hee'l put;

Freckles i'th' face he cures, and takes off Pimples,

'Hath taught me to the ufe of Herbs and Simples.

But I muft beg my fellow-Servant's Pardon,

'Gainft Love there is no Herb nor Flow'r i'th
                                      (Garden:

For this Difeafe I muft rely upon ye,

Come and live here again, you'l cure *Oenone.*

---- ----

PENELOPE

PENELOPE to ULYSSES,

Lately tranflated out of

O V I D

Now BURLESQU'D.

The ARGUMENT.

There hapning a Rebellion in Scotland, in that Army which went under the Command of the Duke ; Ulyffes went Voluntier. The Rebels being quell'd, the Army return'd home ; but Ulyffes lay loitring at fome Inn on the Road ; which when his Careful Wife Penelope underftood, fhe fent him this E-piftle ; giving him an Account how Affairs ftood at home

YOur poor *Penelope* admires that you

Should ever ufe a Woman as you do !

Now

Now every Soldier's at his own aboad,

You, like a Sot, lye tipling on the Road:

   You are not left behind 'em as a Spy,

T' inform, in cafe of fecond Mutiny:

The Devil of Hell will have that Fellow furely,

Who firft began this Plaguy Hurly-burly,

Had it not been for this unlucky Fight,

Y ad ftuck to work all day :---- to me at night.

   Poor I muft drudge at home all forts of weather

And kit,----as Heaven and Earth would come to-
                     (gether;

Twirling a Wheele, I fit at home---hum-drum,

And fpit away my Nature on my Thumb:

Thus while I fpin, you, like a carefull Spoufe,

Go reeling up and down from houfe to houfe.

Being you ftaid fo long I did conjecture,

You had been maul'd by *Sauny*, the *Scotch* Hector:

Old *Neftor's* Son, that Fool, ftood juft by you,

When's empty kcull, they fay, was fpilt in two:

                      And

And, when he dropt, for all you are fo ftout,
You wifh'd your felf at home, in fhitten clout.
Yet after all, *Ulyffes*, I am glad
You are a live, though you're a fcurvy Lad.

Our Neighbours here all day do tittle tattle,
And talk of nothing elfe but Blood and Battle ;
Were you at home, you could not chufe but laugh
To hear 'em crack and bounce, now they are fafe :
Perhaps when three or four of them are met,
And round about a Kitchin-Table fet,

there's fuch a Noife a Clutter, and a Din,
The Rebel *Scots* are routed o're agen.

Some with Tobacco-Pipes upon a Table,
Do valiantly demonftrate to the Rabble
The Foes chief Strength; with that another Spark
Hamilton's Houfe defcribes; a third, the Park ;
Another fpils fome Ale upon the Bench,
And, with his Finger, learns you to entrench ;

One

One acts how fierce our valiant Soldiers ran on,
Difmounts a Can, and tells you 'tis a **Cannon**;
Another cries Neighbours, obferve and look,
This Pot's Sir *Thomas*; and this Glafs the Duke.
Thus while the Husband draws this bloody Scheme,
The Wives behind their Chairs, were in a Dream;
Nay, fome of 'em (I queftion whether'ts true)
Do tell fome mighty Deeds perform'd by you;
That, being provok'd, you like a valiant man drew,
And cut a *Scotch*-man's Luggs off by St. *Andrew.*

   I'm ne'er the nearer, though they'reover-come;
If you'll not mind your Bus'nefs here at Home:
For my own part, I would not care a pinn
If they were ftill in Arms, and you in mine:
Py'thee, come home; I cannot chufe but wonder
What a God's-name you can be doing yonder:
By every Poft and Carrier to the North
I've fent more Paper than your Neck is worth:

               G   I've

I've ſent to *Hull,* to *Berwick,* and to *Grantham* ;

I might as well have ſent a Poſt to *Bantam.*

Perhaps ſome Tapſter's Wife ſubdues your Heart,

Or elſe her Drink's ſo ſtrong you cannot part :

And, when you're drunk, Lord, how your Ton-
(gue does run,

That you've a Houſe well furniſh'd here in Town,

In which your Wife(or rather, Drudge) doth dwell

As conſtantly at home, as Snail in Shell.

(But yet, when I remember parting Kiſſes,

Then,then,methinks thou ſhouldſt be true,*Ulyſſes.*)

My Father ſays you're drow'd i'th watry Main ;

The old Man joques, and bids me wed again ;

His Counſel, like himſelf is ſtill unſound,

I'd rather he were hang'd than you were drown'd.

Every day here comes a ſort of Fellows,

Enow to make a fooliſh Husband jealous,

From *Whetſton's-*Park, *Moor-fields,* or ſuch like
(places

Fellows with Cuts and Frenches in their Faces ;
Ther

There are but seven Fingers amongst four,
And here they domineer, and swear, and roar:
Two of 'em say, they have been vast Commanders,
The other trail'd a Pike with you in *Flanders*;
There's one of 'em, they call him, Merry *Robert*,
He, in a merry way, broke up the Cubboard;
Here hath been *Irus* too, that *Irish* Thief,
W' hath eaten up a Surloin of Roast-Bief;
What signifies my Father or my self,
We can't secure our Meat upon the Shelf?
What great defence can Nurse or little Boy-make
Against a Fellow with a Horses stomach?
The little Rogue your Son, was almost drown'd,
Padling about he tumbled in the Pond,
But we recover'd him with much ado,
I hope he'll prove a better Man than you.

In short, If speedily you do not come,
You will be eaten out of house and home:

G 2   The

The old Man's crazy, we from him muſt part;
And I have lay'd your uſage ſo to heart,
That I am grown ſo wither'd now with Grief,
I look——more like your Mother than——

Your faithful Wife,

PENELOPE.

PHÆDRA

PHÆDRA to HIPPOLYTUS.

The ARGUMENT.

Theseus *having made his Escape out of* France *with* Phædra——(*whose Sister* Ariadne *he deserted at* Calais) *when he came into* England *marry'd her, and brought her home to a Farm-House near* Putney *in* Surrey, *which he Rented of one Mr.* Jove; *which House during his Travell, (or rather his Ramble) he committed to his Son* Hippolytus, *who was a great Hunter, a hansome Fellow, and a Woman---hater ; for which two last Reasons* Phædra *his Mother after she had acquainted her self with her Neighbours, and houshold affairs, fell desperately in Love ; insomuch that nothing would serve her but carnal copulation with her Son in-Law ; to accomplish which she humbly entreats him by this Letter to consider her Condition.*

TO you my Lad, I send this amorous Scroul,

 Wishing you health, with all my Heart and
          (Soul ;

Your Mother, and your Lover does beseech,

That with these Lines you wou'd not wipe your
           (Breech:

Thank God, my Father gave his Children breed-
(ing,
And taught us all, our Writing and our Reading.

By Letters Men have News, and Women find
Which way and how their Sweet-hearts are en-
(clin'd.

Thrice I refolv'd to tell you all I thought,
But for my Blood I cou'd not get it out:

I juft began to fay——My deareft *Poll*,
Then laugh'd, and turn'd afide, and ruin'd all;

Tho' 'tis no laughing matter, for I own
I love the very Ground thou tread'ft upon.

I'll tell thee, *Poll*, and mark me what I fay,
If Love thou Sullenly doft difobey,

Tho' he's a Boy, not half fo big as you,
Yet Fairy-like he'll pinch yo' black and blew;

On a full fpeed your Horfe he'll lead aftray,
And like a Hare he'll crofs you in your way.

If he affaults——you cannot beat him him off
Either with hunting Pole or Quarter-Staff.

'Hath sworn, (tho' to your Father I am wed,)

To bind you fast, and bring you to my Bed.

'Tis true, your strength is great, his only Art,

You pitch the Bar, and he can throw a Dart,

What need I use these words? dear *Polly*—come

Let us embrace, your's not at home.

You know my Reputation's very great,

Whoo'd guess that You and I shou'd do the feat.

Oh how I'am stung, I have as little Ease,

As if I had distrub'd a Hive of Bees.

I purre and purre, just like our Tabby Cat,

As if I knew not what I wou'd be at:

When Young, I cou'd have cur'd these am'rous
(stings

With Carrots, Radishes, or such like things;

Now there's no pleasure in such Earthly cures,

I must have things apply'd as warm as yours.

Where lies the blame, art thou not strong, and
(young?

Who wou'd not gather fruit that is well hung?

G 4   Or

Or who can call't a Sin when we have done,

Main't I have leave to hug my Husband's Son ?

Suppofe our Landlord *Jove,* that gallant Wight,

Had a months mind to lodge with me one night ;

Nay——if his Lady too fhould give confent,

For you I'd quit him, though hee'd quit his rent.

Since you'l not hunt in this my fofter place,

Where I fhould get the better of the chafe ;

Since the large Fields and Woods you rummage,
    (through,

Difdaining my poor little Cunny——borough ;

I'll follow you o're Ditches, and throu' Boggs,

And whoop and hollow after all the Dogs:

I'll fpeak to th' hounds fo well hey ! *Jowler, Bow.*
    (*man,*

That none, but you fhall know I am a Woman:

I'll praife your Greyhound *Delia,* when you courfe,

She fhall my Miftrefs be, and 'Ill be yours.

Under a hedge I'll fquat down like a Hare,

And you alone fhall find me fitting there.

Some-

Sometimes upon a Horse I'll get aftride,

And after you, as I were mad I'll ride;

For all our Generation have been fo,

When they're in Love they know not what they
(do

You've heard that Miftrefs *Europe* was my Gran-
(dam;

She went away with *Jupiter* at Random.

Pafiphae my Mother was fo full

Of ftrange Vagaries that fhe fuck'd a Bull.

My Husband with my Sifter lay—or rather

I fhould have told you it was your Father.

Poor *Adne* was ftarke mad for him, and now

I am (God knows) as mad in Love with you.

So that between the Father and the Son,

There are two Sifters like to be undone.

I never fhall forget with what a Grace

You dreft your felf in order for the chafe;

Your Vifage not too red, but only tan'd,

Of the fame colour with your brawny hand.

An

An ancient Bever on your head you put,

Like a three——Pigeon Pye, in corners cut.

A little Jacket made of blewish green,

Which had the Death of many a Badger feen.

Your hair your own, which shew'd you not de-
(bauch'd,

Not nicely trim'd, for here and there 'twas notch'd.

I hate your Fellows with your powder'd Wigs,

As m' Husband us'd to fay, they look like Prigs.

You'd lasting Breeches made of Buckskin Leather,

To keep the fundamental parts from weather.

But when you reach'd your hanger from the Bed,

Another Weapon came into my head.

Not all your days can give you fuch delight,

Or half the Sport I'll shew you in a Night,

Delia's your Joy, Delia does you bewitch;

Can you neglect a Christian, for a Bitch?

Cephalus your Companion and old Crony,

Valu'd a Dog better than ready money.

Hee'd get upon a Horfe, though half afleep,

Ready to hunt before the Day did peep ;

But when h'ad once tafted *Aurora's* fweets,

He found out better Game between the fheets ;

For then unlefs fhe pleas'd, he durft not fay,

(Nor did he wifh) that it would e're be day.

Why fhould not we confent to try our skill?

I'm certain you and I can do as well.

Therefore dear *Poll*, I offer very fair,

Under *Barn-Elmes* I'll meet you if you dare ;

Since none but Country Sports can humour you,

I'll wraftle wi'll you there a fall or two ;

Though o' my, Confcience I believe you'l throw
(me,

But if you fhou'd, perhaps it won't undo me ;

And when you have me down among the Trees,

You wanton Rogue, you may do what you pleafe.

Wee'd no fuch opportunity before :

Your Father is at *London* with his Whore.

There-

Therefore I think 'tis but a juſt deſign,

To cuckold him, and pay him in his coin.

Beſides he ne're was marry'd to your Mother,

He firſt whor'd her, and then he took another.

What kindneſs or reſpect ought we to ha ve

For ſuch a Villain and perfidious Knave ?

This ſhould not trouble, but provoke us rather

With all the ſpeed we can to lye together.

I am no kin to you, nor you to me,

They call it Inceſt but to terrifie.

Lovers Embraces are Laſcivious Tricks,

'Mongſt muſty Puritans and Schiſmaticks.

Did not our Maſter *Jove* chuſe him a Miſtreſs,

Who ſhould it be but one of his own Siſters ?

There's no engendring can be truely good,

But when we fancy that we are of a blood.

Under the names of Mother and of Son,

What pretty pleaſant actions may be done ?

Al

All they will fay, becaufe I'm kind to thee,

I'm Mother both in Law and Equity:

Take heart of Grace, be not afraid of Spyes,

I care not if there were Ten thoufand Eyes;

I'll leave the door without the Bolt or Lock:

What if they faw us in our Shirt or Smock.

Nay I'll fuppofe we fhould be feen in Bed,

What can there to our prejudice be faid?

That you came wet and dripping from the chafe,

And I'd a mind to give you my warm place.

I did not think to've faid fo much in haft,

But Love like Murder muft come out at laft:

The Fort lies open, therefore fcorn it not,

But come with fpeed, and enter on the fpot;

Let us imagine now the worft can happen;

Suppofe that you and I were taken napping;

And *Thefeus* fays, Begone you filthy Whore;

Away you Rogue, and fo he fhuts the door.

What

What if he does, why then for *France* with ſpeed,

We ſhall be there ſupply'd with all we need.

My Father dwells at *Paris* in good credit,

And well to paſs is he, though I have ſaid it ;

There he's as well known as Begger knows his diſh,

We'll live as bravely then as Heart can wiſh :

Therefore make haſte, dream not of any harms,

Thou'lt be ſecure enough within my arms.

When you go out, may you be ſure of Game ;

May your horſe never tire nor happen lame :

At a default may the Dogs never be,

May *Delia* bring forth Whelps as good as ſhe.

May you i'th' Field ne're want a draught of Beer,

Or Bread and Cheeſe, or ſuch like hunting cheer;

While I ſit pining for you here at home,

When I have cry'd out both my Eyes you'l come.

HYPSIPYLE.

HYPSIPYLE to JASON.

Lately Tranflated out, of

O V I D:

Now BURLESQU'D.

The ARGUMENT.

Jafon, a quondam *Foot-man,* with fome others, the nimbleft of the fame Function, joyn'd their Stocks, and purchas'd a *Silver-Bowl,* which they ran for from Barnet *to* St. Albans ; *but before the day of the Match,* one Medæa, *a* Gipfey, *and* Strouler *in* thofe Parts, took a more than ordinary fancy towards Jafon, whom fhe fo dieted with new laid Eggs, or what the Devil it was elfe, (fhe being fufpected of Witchcraft,) that he won the Plate ; and beat two famous Foot Jockeys, Whipping- Tom and Teage : Hypfipyle, his Wife, whom
he

*he had deserted, hearing of his good success, and
withall, of his Love-intrigue with* Medæa, *caused
this Epistle to be sent to him.*

From So-hoe *Fields*, Feb. 27. 16$\frac{79}{80}$.

Husband,

THE Neighbours in our Alley do relate,
   That at St. *Albans* you have won the Plate.
How easie a matter had it been for you.
T'have sent poor *Hyp.* your Wife, a *George* or two?
   Did I, when *Flannel* was both dear and scarce,
Make you Trunk-hose to your ungrateful Arse;
I sew'd so long, my Fingers still do ake,
And, in all Conscience, I deserve my Snack.
   I can hear something, though I keep at home;
I hear, y'have beaten *Teague* and *Whipping-Tom.*
You ran so swift, and strong, the People say,
You bore down all that stood but in your way:

Befor

Before your foundred Fellows could come up
You won the Match, and feis'd the *Caudla-Cup.*
I know, y' have been a Rogue, and done me
(wrong;
Yet I'd hear this from your own flattring Tongue.
But why fhouldft thou e'er hope for that, poor
(*Hypfi,*
Since *Jafon* loves a Bacon-vifag'd Gipfey.
As I was wafhing, th'other day at door,
There came a Scoundril, ill-look'd Son-of-a-whore,
Who, jeering, ask'd if I were Madam *Jafon* ?
I'd like t'have thrown Soap fuds his ugly Face-on,
Said I, I'm *Jafon*'s Wife, for want of better ;
Have you brought Money, from him, or a Letter?
How does he do ? is he not very fine ?
Come, come, let's fee, I'm fure h'ath fent me Coin.
Quoth he, By God of Heaven, not a Souze ;
He only bid me fee you at your Houfe.
The Fellow told m' a Tale of Cock and Bull ;
At laft, I ask'd about your Tawny-Trull.

H   He

He faid, *Medea*'s your beloved Gipfey,
And that your often feen together tipfey;
But, he believ'd 'twas but a Trick of youth :
A Trick; faid I, the Devil ftop your Mouth.
  Wound I had been lafh'd and wihipt the City
                                        (round
That day I marry' thee, loofe Vagabond :
The Hangman in difguife read Common-pray'r
When we were match'd, a very Hopefull Pair :
Curft be the time I did admit you firft,
And ftrove to quench your everlafting thirft :
What Plague poffeft me when I brought you
                                        home?
This was no place to run with *Whipping-Tom*,
  If I had taken but my Sifters counfel,
Y'had never fet your flat-foot o'er the grou ndfel :
She bid me exercife the Fork and Spit ;
We'd then good Goods, but now the De'il a bit,
  'i was well enough a year, nay, almoft two;
What Fury hath poffeffion of you now ?
                                        Villain,

Villain, remember when you went away,

How often you Damn'd your felf, you would not
(ftay;

And fmoothly faid, No place fhall us divide;

A Curfe upon your bafe diffembling Hide:

I was fo big that I could hardly tumble,

Yet I believ'd your Oaths, and durft not grumble:

Said you, dear *Hypfi.* know that I am dead,

If I don't come before you're brought to bed;

You look'd like Air, with Breeches clofe to thighs,

I fancy'd you'd be back within a trice:

When you were gone I to the Garret crept,

To fee how nimbly o'er the Fields you tript;

As fwift you went, fo fwift return you'ld make,

But all this hafte was for that Bitche's fake:

Why do I rub my windows, wafh my Room,

Expecting ftill your Roguefhip would come home?

'Twould never vex me, if you were not feen

With fuch a damn'd confounded nafty Quean:

A Witch, a Bitch, in whom the Devil dwells,
Whofe Face is made of Greafe and Wall-nut-fhells.
Mafter, quoth fhe, e'er from this Town you ftir
You'll lofe, (that is Your Pocket's pick'd by her.)
A plaguy Jade, who curfes Night and Noon,
And houls, and heaves her Arfe againft the Moon,
Contemning her as Authrefs of the Flowers;
Railing at all our Sex, and Poxing yours:
No Childing Women doth in Travel linger,
But tow'rds her Pain the Fiend holds up a Finger:
She'll ride a Stick ; when Sow is brought to bed,
Then Pigs have no more life than pigs of Lead:
She, with the Mother, at a door will wheedle,
And, in her Infant's heart, will ftick a Needle:
This I believe, what e'er of me you think,
S' hath put fome Rotten-poft into your drink.

'Tis ftrange, that I fhould fuffer all thefe wrongs
From her whom I would fcorn to touch with
(Tongs.
. You'll

You'll lofe the Name of beating *Tom* and *Teague*,

Whilft with this Whore you do continue League :

Nay, fome do very confidently fay't,

'Twas by her Witch-craft that you won the Plate :

Some think her Devil, others, new-laid Eggs,

Made you fo faft advance your Bandy-leggs :

What can you find in fuch a Punck as fhe

Who from a Dunhill brings her Pedigree ?

My Father dwells at Sign of *Golden-Can*,

An honeft Vict'ler, a fubftantial Man :

'Tis true, they fay, he is a drunken Sot ;

What then ; i'th' Parifh he paies Scot and Lot :

Old *Bacchus*, the Wine-cooper, was my Grandfire;

Let her produce fuch Kindred if fhe can Sir :

Her Children have been gotten in a Bog.

By fome large-pintled Wolf, or Maftive Dog :

My Babes were neither got nor whelp'd i'th'
(Streets,

I labour'd for them 'twixt a pair of Sheets :

H 3   That

That they are yours, I'm fure, you need not
(doubt,
For they're as like as if y' had fpit them out:
Could they have gone, alone I'd made 'em amble
To your Apartment underneath a Bramble;
But I confider'd how your Whore would treat
('em,

Nay, it is ten to one, the Hag would eat 'em;
Or elfe, perhaps, fhe'd ftick their tender Skins
All full of Sparables, or croocked Pins;
Since of her own s' hath murther'd many a Brat,
Would fhe fpare mine; oh ! never tell me that.
Methink I fee you and the hell-born Toad
Engendring in a Tree that's near the Road:
Suppofe you were purfu'd, as y' are a Thief;
Where would you fly ? where would you find
(relief?
What if your felf and yonder Devil's dam
Should come to me, and try if you could fham?

Sure

Sure I fhould make you very welcome both,

And entertain you nobly by my Troth.

I fhould towards you make fome relenting
                                        (Heart,
But 'tis my Goodnefs more than your defert:

And, for your Fire-brand there, that loathfome
                                        (Hag,
I would contrive the greateft Pain and Plague:

Her Nofe being flit, to make her look more grim,

Like a *Spred-Eagle* on her Face fhould feem:

Her coarfe black Skin fhould from her Flefh be
                                        (rent;
I'd run a Spit into her Fundament:

And, *Jafon*, this thy Punifhment fhould be,

Thou fhouldft eat thofe, fo oft have fwallow'd
                                        (thee.

But fince it muft not be I am contented

To let my Spleen in curfing her be vented:

May fhe all Suftenance for ever lack,

Untill fhe takes her Child from off her Back,

And puts it in her belly for a Nuncheon,

And for the Fact be thrown into a Dungeon:

                    H 4   May

May she be burnt to Cinders as a Witch,
And you be hang'd for loving of a Bitch.

Yours, as you have us'd her,

HYPSIPYLE.

For John Jason, *to be left at his Apartment, in a hollow Tree, between* Barnet *and* St. Albans.

PARIS

PARIS to *HELLEN.*

The ARGUMENT.

Paris had liv'd a great while in Obscurity, at last being own'd by Alderman Priam *a Rich Old Citizen, and receiv'd as his Son----he set up for a Gentleman; but very well knowing he could not be rightly accomplish'd without a Mistress, and hearing Fame speak* viva voce *in the praise of one* Hellen, *who liv'd somewhere in the* North. *He was at her house receiv'd, and during the absence of* Menelaus *her Husband, he endeavour'd to break his Mind to her; but being not thorough-pac'd in Gentility, his Modesty got the the upper hand of his Inclination, therefore he presently had recourse to his Pen, and writes her this conceited Letter.*

FReely and from my heart without compel-
(ling,

I wish all health and happiness to *Hellen*:

For if yur're Sick, I'm sure to suffer pain;

As I'm a Lover and a Gentleman,

I need

I need not tell you that I'm off oth' hooks,
Your Ladiſhip diſcerns it by my Looks:
For you whoſe Eyes have ſuch a piercing-quick-
(neſs,
May ſee I'm overgrown in the Green-ſickneſs;
So that upon the whole and perfect Matter,
I am your ſervant but I ſeem your Daughter.
I cou'd eat walls as well as white bred crum,
But fear to eat you out of houſe and home.
For this diſtemper I've read many Cures,
But the ſole power of healing muſt be Yours.
Your Holineſs (I cannot call you leſs,
That doth on Earth perform ſuch Miracles,)
Your holineſs I ſay within few weeks,
May fetch a lively colour in my Cheeks.
But if we are to long e're we begin,
I'm apt to fear it may corrupt within.
'Tis Love, 'tis Love, that makes me toſs & tumble,
And in my Entrails does like Jollup rumble:

'Tis

'Tis as impoſſible you ſhould not ſee't,

As 'tis to hide the Pox both ſmall and great.

'Tis Love, You know th' effects of that diſeaſe,

Therefore pray fall to work when e're you pleaſe,

If at theſe Lines you do not jeer nor Jybe,

There is ſome hopes you may receive the Scribe.

And Madam know, I did engage the Stars,

Before I durſt engage in *Cupid*'s Wars.

This is a grand affair, I had been ſilly

T'ave ventur'd on't whithout conſulting *Lilly* :

To him I went for my own happy ends,

And all the Planets he hath made my Friends,

But above all, the moſt pellucid *Venus*,

Hath promis'd there ſhould be a Job between us :

She knoweth beſt what's good for you and me,

She does command our Fates and Powers d'ye ſee.

Without her leave no living Lover ſtirs,

Paris, ſaid ſhe, put on your Boots and Spurs.

She

She did confent I fhould afcend my horfe,

And toward your Manfion bend my glorious
(courfe.

Never by her was riding yet forbidden,

Her Goddefs-fhip with pleafure has been ridden.

My heart's upon the racking trot----alas!

But fhe can bring it to a Gentle pace.

Next, Madam, know, your Sight was no fuprize,

I lov'd you by my Ears as well as Eyes.

Your Fame hath much out-founded the Report,

Of the great Guns at taking of a Fort.

I came not here to feek terreftial pelf,

I made this progrefs for your heavenly felf.

The Womb o'th' Univerfe if I fhould rifle,

'To your more fecret parts 'twere but a trifle.

To fee your ancient Pile, I do not range,

We have more lofty Fabricks near th' Exchange.

'Twas for your fake I fpurr'd my ftubborn Steed,

For you alone thro' thick and thin I rid.

You're

You're mine, what defperate mortal dares gain-
(fay't?
Sure I may take my Planet's word for that.

I fain would tell your Ladifhip a Dream,

If it would not too great a trouble feem.

My Mother dream't, when fhe with me was quick,

She fhould bring forth a lighted Fagot---ftick :

I am that Fagot-ftick, I burn a pace,

Oh quench me, Madam, in your watring---place.

I've taken fire at you, as a match at tinder ;

Cool me, or elfe your Servant is a Cinder.

This was my Mother's dream, I now defign,

Under Correction, to relate your mine.

   I laid me down to fleep one Summers day,

Under the fhade of a new Stack of Hay ;

For we poor Lovers, fuch is our hard cafe,

Are glad to take a Nap in any place ;

Three naked Ladies came, I well remember,

As naked as the Trees are---in *December* ;

                       They

They told me they'd be judg'd alone by me,

Which was the moft deferving of the Three ;

The firft would bribe me with a Purfe of Gold ;

My Judgment's neither to be bought nor fold :

The fecond offer'd me a Tilting Sword,

Knowing I ne're would take an angry word :

But fayes the third, and in my face fhe giggled,

With fuch poor toyes you're not to be inveigled,

But if you value me above the reft,

Then know young---man, you are for ever bleft.

Within a little time you fhall arrive,

Where a refplendent Country Dame does live ;

Firft you muft court her like an humble Beggar,

At laft fhee'll yield, and you may lay your Leg---
                                                  (o're ;

The Prize is yours, faid I, you ought to take't,

I kifs'd her lower Parts, and fo I wak'd.

My Dream is out, for thus I do explain it,

You are the Countrey Dame, and fhe the Planet.

Without

Without delay I put on my accoutring,
And with full speed, I came to you----a----fuitring.
But juft as I was putting Foot in Stirrup,
Drinking with Friends a parting cup of Syrrup,
My Sifter came to th' door, a mad young Lafs,
Her name's *Caffandra*, but we call her *Cafs*;
Brother, quoth fhe, beware, beware, I fay,
You do not meet a Firefhip by the way:
A ftrange wild Wench, I hope fhe did not mean
That any where your Ladifhip's unclean;
Heavens forbid, Good Soul, fhe meant no more
Then flames of Love, as I have faid before.
Being arriv'd at this your decent houfe,
Whom fhould I meet but your Illuftrious Spoufe?
He brought a Tankard out of good March Beer,
Cold Pork and Butter, and fuch houfhold chear;
He ask'd----if ever I Tobacco took,
I faid I'd take a pipe----but cou'd not fmoak;

He

He fhew'd m' his Garden, and his fine young
(Trees,
His Barn, his Stable, and his houfe of Eafe :
I faid 'twas wondrous pretty----but my mind
Still ran on what my Planet had defign'd.
At laft you came with fuch a dazling grace,
I thought the Sun and Moon was in your face,
Lilly's and Rofes, Pinks and Violets,
Your looks were loaded with the vernal fweets ;
Your poor adorer was in fuch amaze,
I vow and fwear I knew not where I was;
Before I fpoke I fell to private pray'r,
" Planet I thank the for thy tender care ;
" Now thou haft rais'd my Blifs to fuch a pitch,
" I humbly beg, that thou'dft go thorough ftitch.
At laft I fpake and bow'd in feemly wife,
And paid obeyfance to your fparkling Eyes ;
Your Beauty's greater than your fame did boaft,
So is a May-Pole taller than a Poft.

Pre

I've heard, you once conferr'd your gracious fa-
(vour
On *Thefeïs*, who was thought a cunning fhaver ;
With him your Ladïfhip has play'd fome Gambols,
Froliques y'have had, and many pleafant rambles;
But, by your Leave, your Lover was a **Clown**,
For leaving your bright Eminence fo foon ;
D'ye think that *Paris* would have ferv'd you fo,
Would he have let Illuftrious *Hellen* go ?
By *Stix* and *Acheron* your Servant fwears,
Rather than part with you, he'll lofe his Ears ;
When that hour comes for which we both were
(born
And foon 'twill come, or Planet is forfworn ;
When we fhall lye entranc'd —— entranc'd I fay,
Then if you have the heart to go, you may ;
Haften, forfooth, haften the happy Job,
For till't be done--— my heart will fhout and
(throb:

I   'Ti

'Tis very fit that you and I fhould join,
Your Family's very good and fo is mine.

My Father fin'd for Alderman, long fince,
He's now grown rich, and lives like any Prince.
If you wou'd once make *London* your aboad.
You'd hate a Village as you'd hate a Toad.
Oh how your Ladifhip wou'd ftare to fee
Our City Dames in all their Bravery.
They've Petticoats with Lace above their knees
Of Gold and Silver, or of Point *Veni-ce* ;
Cornets and lofty Tow'rs upon the head,
And wondrous fhapes of which you never read.
How ill a Pinner with a narrow Lace,
Becomes the Beauty of fo bright a Face ?
A fairer Face no mortal e're laid Lips to,
And I believe there are not whiter Hips too.
Too white to mingle with a Husband's thighes,
When I but think of that, my flefh does rife.

When

When towards me fometimes a Glance does pafs,
Your poor Adorer looketh like an Afs.
For if I fhould return you Look for Look,
I fear your Husband will begin to fmoak ;
And I'll be hang'd, if ever *Menelaus*,
By any am'rous Look of mine, betray us ;
Were it not at your Table I'd abufe him,
For thrufting his great Paw into your Bofom :
That Watry Fift between your Breaft does feem
Like a brown *George* dropt in a Bowl of Cream.
I'm mad to fee him draw his Chair fo clofe,
And kifs, and hugg you underneath my Nofe.
Then I go out, pretending to make Water,
Seeming to take no notice of the matter :
To all true Hearts I drink a Cup of Wine,
A Health that does imply both yours and mine ;

Then

Then feeming drunk, I tell fome ftrange Romance,

And lay the Scene in *Italy* or *France* ;

Of fome bright Lady, and her brisk----Gall----ant;

By which two Lovers, you and I are meant.

But, Madam, to write more of this were non-
(fence,

My Planet has contriv'd the bus'nefs long-fince ;

By curious fearch I fomething can difcover,

'Tis in your Blood---you're born to be a Lover.

What think you Lady, of your Father *Jove*?

Shew me a Town-bull h'as been more in Love.

Your Mother, *Leda*, too, who gave you fuck,

H'as fhe not been as good as ever ftruk ?

When s'had a lufty Youth between her thighs,

What d'ee think ? would *Leda* cry to rife ?

Your Parents being as right as ever pift,

If you fhould be precife, you wou'd be hift.

But

But if you muſt be conſtant to óne Man,

With me to *London* make what haſt you can.

There wee'll provide a little Winter Houſe,

And you ſhall paſs for my renowned Spouſe.

By what I ſee your Husband does approve,

That in your Abſence here I ſhould make Love.

Or wou'd he elſe have gone,——under pretence,

To buy a Horſe---a hundred miles from hence?

The Buſ'neſs ſeems to me, as plain a caſe,

As is the Noiſe upon your beauteous face.

To let you know that I ſhould be no clog,

Did he not ſay, Love me and love my Dog?

Nelly, ſaid he, be kind unto my Gueſt,

And let his entertainment be the *Beſt.*

I preſently his meaning underſtood,

If yours be not the *Beſt*---then nothing's good.

You ſee your Husband orders our affairs,

Therefore, dear Madam, do not hang an Arſe,

But

But let's away to *London*----*Crop* does wait,

Saddled and bridled at the Garden----gate ;

Crop's a good Natur'd Beaſt----and carries double,

And will not think your Ladiſhip a trouble.

Strike while the Iron's hot, my Love is fervant,

Get up, and ride behind——

Your humble Servant

Paris.

HELLEN's

HELLEN's Anſwer to PARIS

The ARGUMENT.

Hellen *having receiv'd his Letter, at firſt ſeems won-*
derfully diſpleas'd at his Impudence, in attempting
a Lady of her unſpotted fame; who was bred and
born in the Town where ſhe liv'd, and was never
call'd Whore. At length the Storm's over, and ſhe
Tacks about, giving him an aſſurance of her readi-
neſs to comply, but doubts her Gallent wo'not be con-
ſtant. In plain Engliſh She's as willing as He.

YOur Letter's wrot in ſuch a filthy ſtile,
    I did not think an anſwer worth my while,

Till I conſidere'd you might offer vi'lence,

And take advantage of a Woman's ſilence.

I'm ſure you have not wanted drink or food,

I wonder in my heart you'll be ſo rude.

I 4   'Tis

'Tis fine y'faith---becaufe you come from *London*,
You think a Country Body muft be run down.
You of your Entertainment here may brag,
You were not us'd as if you'd had the Plague.
My Husband did receive you as a *Friend*,
And wou'd you to his Wife now prove a *Fiend*?
Perhaps you'll fay of me, when you are gone,
Hellen! a Lady !——*Hellen*'s but a clown.
I'll one the name, fince you can fay no more,
I'd rather be a Clown, then call'd a Whore:
Yet for all that, though I keep Cows and Daries,
I can behave my felf as well as *Paris*.
Tho' I don't fleer like a young wanton Girle,
Yet you fhall feldom fee me frown or fnarle.
Tho' you fuch breeding, and fuch manners own,
Let me deal plainly w'ye----I think you've none.
Or could you elfe believe me fo untrue,
To leave my Spoufe and run away with you ?

Becaufe

Becaufe a Fellow once did pick me up,
You think I'm to be ftoln by every Fop.
He knew not whether I was Man or Woman,
But you conclude from thence that I am common.
When he perceiv'd *that I was none of thofe*,
He very fairly brought me to my houfe.
And fince I'm gotten quit of Mafter *Thefeus*,
Our *Paris* wou'd be nibbling too, God blefs us !----
Though by my Trooth I cannot blame your Love,
If I were fure that you wou'd conftant prove,
Dy'e think I fhould not be in dainty pickle,
If I fhould run away with one that's fickle?
You urg'd to me th' example of my Mother,
As if the Daughter fhou'd be fuch another.
You don't confider *Leda*, was betray'd,
By one that courted her in Mafquerade.
She thought fh'ad met a harmlefs plum of feather,
But at *long-run* he prov'd a Stallion rather.

                                        His

His Famili's the beſt in all the County,
All that you live by's but a Tradſman's bounty.
But that's all one, whereever love prevails,
Money's no more than pairing of my Nails.
Sometimes I think you love me when you look
With Eyes unmov'd, juſt like a Pig that's ſtuck.
And dabble with your fingers in my Palm,
And uſe to call the moiſture of it, —Balm.
If in the Glaſs I leave a little drop,
You'd ſay I'll drink your ſnuffs—and ſuck it up.
Hellen you carv'd with Penkife on the Gate,
And I wrot *Paris juſt a top* of that.
Theſe are ſhrewd ſigns of Love, and without
(doubt,
You'd give a Leg or Arm to have a Bout.
Tho' you are not the firſt Man by a hundred,
That has ſeen me, and lov'd and gaz'd and won-
(dred.
If you at firſt had come into our Town,
And courted *Hellen* in a Grogram Gown,

When

When I was but a filly Soul, God knows,

You might have made a Bridge of *Menel*'s Nofe.

Now he commands in chief your Suit is vain,

To all true Lovers Marriage is a Bane.

But why fhould *Paris* for a Miftrefs long,

Since in your Sleep your Fancy is fo ftrong?

You can fee three ftark naked at a time,

And take your choice of Beauty's in a dream:

Yet you left Honour, Wealth, and God knows
                      (what.

And all for me—a pretty fancy that.

I know 'tis wheedle, —— but if all were true,

It is no more than I would do for you.

You guefs my want of Skill, by being fo plain,

For I'am not us'd to write to any Man,

Except t' a Millener, (my Husband's Cozen)

Who fends me Gloves, —— and Ribbands by the
                      (dozen.

Well—— fince it muft be fo——let's be difcreet,

Let not our Town take notice that we meet;
                      For

For they fufpect already you're a Wencher,
There is not fuch a place on Earth for Cenfure
Yet I can't fee, why we fhould be fo nice,
I like you----by my Husband's own advice.
I cou'd not chufe but laugh to hear him fay,
Pray Love your Gueft when I am gone away :
And all the while that *Menelaus* tarries.
You are committed to the charge of *Paris.*
The charge ! Let us examine well the word,
Whether he meant your charge at Bed and Board;
Why fhould he not mean both as well as one ?
He knows----how much I hate to lye alone.
In my weak Judgment, 'tis an eafie Cafe,
You are in all things to fupply his place.
But for the Mafterfhip you're like to tug
Before you have me at the clofeft hug.
,Twill feem to me, if you fome force do ufe,
As if I had a Maidenhead to lofe.

Lord !

Lord ! how I write ; if I were to be damn'd,

I cou'd not fay't —— I fhould be fo afham'd.

If I confent I'll hold you any Money,

You'll ferve me as you did you'r dear *Oenone.*

She hop'd fhe fhould be wedded in the Church,

Inftead of that you left her in the Lurch.

But if we now were toward *London* jogging,

'Tis ten to one fome Puppy would be dogging,

Or elfe fome Neighbour on the Read wou'd ftay
(us,

And ask me after Mr. *Menelaus.*

Or we fhall hear the Country-people fay,

Would you believe that fhe fhould run-away ?

Marry not hanfome Wives by this Example,

Since pretty Miftrefs *Hellen*'s on the Ramble

I'm ftrangly afraid of feeing Mr. *Priam,*

How I fhall tremble when he asks whom I----am.

Tho' for my Life I fhall not hold from Laughter,

If *Hecuba,* fhould fay Your Servant, Daughter

But

But above All 'tis *Hector* that I dread,
That *Hector* certainly will break my Head.
Who'd think you two from the fame Mother
(came,
He's like a Lyon, you are like a Lamb.
Let *Hector* profer with his fenfelefs huffing,
'Tis *knowing nothing now* that makes a Ruffian,
While *Paris* fhall be skill'd in Lovers Arts,
And dive into our Sexes fecret Parts ;
Now you begin to think 'tis ten to one,
Your Suit is granted, and the Bus'nefs done.
But not fo faft, —— confult my Friend *Clymene*,
No doubt—you'l make the Bus'nefs up between
(ye
I'm loath to fay't my felf, fhe knows my mind,
And fhe can tell you how I am enclin'd.
When fhe informs you what muft be tranfacted,
With too much Joy, I fear, you'l run diftracted.

F I N I S.

THe Hiftories and Novels of the late Inge-nious Mrs. *Behn* collected in on Volume, *viz. Oronoko*: Or the Royal Slave. The fair Jilt: Or Prince *Tarquine*. *Agnes de Caftro*: Or the Force of Generous Love. Loves Watch: Or the Art of Love. The Ladies Lookinglafs. The Lucky Miftake, and Letters never before Printed, with the Life and Memoirs of Meftrifs *Behn*. Written by on of the fair Sex, *Price* 4 *s.*

Sir *Sam. Moreland*'s *Vade Mecum*: Or the Ne-ceffary Companion. Containing, 1. A Perpetual Almanack, readily fhewing the Day of the Month, and Moveable Feafts and Terms, for any Year paft, prefent, or to come, curioufly graved in Copper; with many ufeful *Tables* proper thereto. 2. The years of each King's Reign from the Nor-man Conqueft compar'd with the Years of Chrift. 3. Directions for every Month in the Year, what is to be done in the Orchard, Kitchin, and Flower-Gardens. 4. The Reduction of Weights, Mea-fures, and Coins; wherein is a Table of the Af-fize of Bread. 5. A Table wherein any Num-ber of Farthings, Half-pence, Pence, or Shillings, are ready caft up; of great ufe to all Traders. 6. The Intereft and Rebate of Money; the For-bearance, Difcompt, and Purchafe of Annuities. 7. The rates of Poft-Letters, both In-land and Out-land. 8. An Account of the Penny-Poft. 9. The

The Principal Roads in *England*, shewing the distance of one Town from another in measured and computed Miles, and the distance of each from *London*; also the Market-Towns, on each Road, with the Days of the Week the Markets are kept on; as likewise the Hundred and County each Town stands in. 10. The Names of the Counties, Cities, and Borough-Towns in *England* and *Wales*, with the Number of Knights, Citizens, and Burgesses chosen therein to serve in Parliament. 11. The usual and authorized Rates of Fairs of Coach-men, Car-men, and Water-men. The Sixth Edition with Tables for casting up Nobles, Marks, Guineas, and Broad Gold.

Cocker's Decimal Arithmitick, The Second Edition, Corrected and Enlarged, by *John Hawkins*.

A new Body of Geography: Or a Description of the Earth, containing by way of Introduction, the General Doctrine of Geography. 2. Description of all the known Countries of the Earth, Account of their Situation, Bounds and Extent. 3. The Principal Cities and most Considerable Towns in the World; particularly an exact Description, &c. 4. Maps of every Country in *Europe*, and a General Map of *Asia*, *Africa* and *Amarica*, fairly Engraven'd on Copper, according to the best and latest Extant: And also particular Draughts of the Chief Fortified Towns of *Europe*: with an Alphabetical Table of the Names of the Places.

RAMBLE:

AN

ANTI-HEROICK

POEM.

Together with

Some Terreſtrial Hymns and Carnal Ejaculations.

By Alexander Radcliffe, *of Greys Inn, Eſq*.

——*Semel inſanivimus omnes.*

LONDON,

Printed for the Author, and are to be ſold by
Walter Davis in Amen Corner. 1682.

TO THE

RIGHT HONOURABLE,

JAMES

Lord Annefly.

My Lord,

THE onely pretence I had
for making this mean Offer
to your Lordſhip is, That your
Lordſhip was pleas'd to excuſe
ſome of theſe looſe Lines when

they were in single Sheets : Tho I must confess I propos'd a great Advantage, knowing that they shall live above the reach of Censure under your Lordships Protection, not without some Ambition of being known to your Lordship by the Title of,

Your Lordships most Humble and most Obedient Servant,

Alex. Radcliffe.

THE
AUTHOR
TO THE
READER.

Honeſt Reader,

IF I thought you would not ſmile immoderately, I cou'd tell you, That by the Command of ſome Honourable Perſonages, Mark ye ! and at the Requeſt of my Noble Friends, D' ye mind me ! theſe Trifles made

a Sally

The Author

a Sally into the World, ſtept into the Light, appear'd in this undreſs, or as a Modern Author has it, was Impetuonſly Hurried into the Preſs, (by which he verified, Feſtinans Canis cœcos peperit catulos.)

This you know is the true Cant of many Prefacers; as who ſhould ſay, Gentlemen, my Book begs your pardon for this Intruſion. But if ſuch kind of Stuff will not paſs as an Excuſe for Publication, I'll tell ye what will; by chance I overheard an offer of ſome fooliſh Guinneys, and

when

when those Toys are propos'd, such is our Human Frailty, we consent to the printing of any thing.

I have not further to say in the behalf of this Affair, since many of these things were wrote several years ago, when Youth and too much Money represented Extravagance a Virtue.

This is the last of this nature I shall ever own; the next shall be some Remarks upon the Life and Death of a true pious Protestant Dissenter, with

the

the *Excellency* and *Necessity* of Per-
jury and *Equivocation* in a devout
Separatist ; and that you'll say is a se-
rious business.

—— Paulo majora canamus.
God b'ye lovingly.

The Bookſellers Preface to his Cuſtomers.

Obliging Gentlemen,

THE Ingenious Author having, next to his pleaſure of writing theſe Poems, taken care to Dedicate them to a Perſon of Honour , and alſo provided an Epiſtle to the Reader, hath left me nothing to do, but for my profit to print and to ſell them. But there having been ſome part of The Ramble *formerly printed, under the notion of a Natural Preſumptive to my Lord* Rocheſter *, for Juſtice to that Noble Lord, as alſo for defending of Liberty and Property to my Author, whoſe Right as well as my own is invaded ; I reſolved to bring an Ha-*

beas

The Bookseller

beas Corpus, *and remove* The Ramble *home again, which was so falsly, maliciously, imperfectly, and feloniously made publick.*

I am likewise to tell you, that the foresaid Poem called The Ramble, *is here enlarged above two thirds more than heretofore you have seen it. I hope it will please you, good honest Gentile Reader ; if so, it will sell ; and if it sells, it will please me too ; and so our little share of the world will naturally run in a concord, without tormenting our selves with Fears and Jealousies, or setting up for mon‑ strous Whigs, Tantivy Tories, Abhorring Ad‑ dressers, or other inferiour no Protestant Plots and Tory Plots. For my part (Gentlemen) I am resolved (nemine contradicente) to live in a whole skin so long as I can, hoping*

no

to the Reader.

no Irishman *will make a dead blow upon me;
and I do hereby promise upon the word of an
honest Stationer, that I will not endeavour
to alter the Government, as it is established
by Law either in Church or State. In fine,
I am satisfied this Book of Poems hath no
couched Treason in it, nor Arbitrary Power,
and therefore I presume to Print it, without
staying for the Suffrage of an Act of Parliament. Such as it is take it amongst you, and
so God bless you all. Vale.*

The

The Contents.

To

The Contents.

POEMS.

POEMS.

News from Hell.

SO dark the Night was that old *Charon*
    Could not carry Ghoftly Fare-on;
    But was forc'd to leave his Souls,
        Stark ftript of Bodies, 'mongft the Shoals
Of Black Sea-Toads, and other Fry,
Which on the Stygian Shore do lie:
Th' amazed Spirits defire recefs
To their old batter'd Carcafes;
But as they turn about, they find
The Night more difmal is behind.

 Pluto began to fret and fume
Becaufe the Tilt Boat did not come.

To the Shore's fide he ftrait way trudges
With his three Soul-cenfuring Judges,
Standing on Acherontic Strand,
He thrice three times did waft his Wand:
From gloomy Lake did ftrait arife
A meager Fiend, with broad blew Eyes;
Approaching *Pluto,* as he bow'd,
From's head there dropt Infernal Mud;
Quoth he, *A tenebris & luto*
I come——'Tis well, quoth furly *Pluto.*
" Go you to t'other fide of *Styx,*
" And know why *Charon's* fo prolix:
" Surely on Earth there cannot be
" A Grant of Immortality.
Away the wrigling Fiend foon fcuds
Through Liquids thick as Soap and Suds.

In the mean while old *Eacus,*
Craftier far than any of us;

For mortal Men to him are filly ;

Befides he held a League with *Lilly* ;

And what is acted here does know

As well as t'other does below :

Thus fpake, " Thou mighty King of *Orcus*,

" Who into any fhape canft work us ;

" I to your Greatnefs fhall declare

" My Sentiments of this Affair.

" *Charon* you know did ufe to come

" With fome Elucid Spirit home ;

" Some Poet bright, whofe glowing Soul

" Like Torch did light him crofs the Pool :

" Old *Charon* then was blithe and merry,

" With Flame and Rhapfody in Ferry.

" Shou'd he grofs Souls alone take in,

" Laden with heavy rubbifh Sin ;

" Sin that is nothing but Allay ;

" 'Tis ten to one he'd lofe his way.

" But now fuch Wights with Souls fo clear

" Muft not have Damnation here ;

Not

" Nor can we hope they'l hither move,

" For know (Grim Sir) they're damn'd above;

" They're damn'd on Earth by th' prefent Age,

" Damn'd in Cabals, and damn'd o'th' Stage.

" *Laureat*, who was both learn'd and florid,

" Was damn'd long fince for filence horrid:

" Nor had there been fuch clutter made,

" But that this filence did invade:

" Invade ! and fo 't might well, that's clear :

" But what did it invade ?——an Ear.

" And for fome other things, 'tis true,

" We follow Fate that does purfue.

A Lord who was in Metre wont

To call a Privy Member C——

Whofe Verfe, by Women termed lewd,

Is ftill preferv'd, not underftood.

But that which made 'em curfe and ban,

Was for his Satyr againft Man.

A third was damn'd, 'caufe in his Plays
He thrufts old Jefts in *Archee*'s days :
Nor as they fay can make a *Chorus*
Without a Tavern or a Whore-houfe ;
Which he to puzzle vulgar thinking,
Does call by th' name of Love and Drinking.

   A fourth for writing fuperfine,
With words correct in every Line :
And one that does prefume to fay,
A Plot's too grofs for any Play :
Comedy fhould be clean and neat,
As Gentlemen do talk and eat.
So what he writes is but Tranflation,
From Dog and Patridge converfation.

   A fifth, who does in's laft prefer
'Bove all, his own dear Character :
And fain wou'd feem upon the Stage
Too Manly for this flippant Age.

A fixth, whofe lofty Fancy towers
'Bove Fate, Eternity and Powers:
Rumbles i'th' Sky, and makes a buftle;
So Gods meet Gods i'th dark and juftle.

Seventh, becaufe he'd rather chufe
To fpoil his Verfe than tire his Mufe.
Nor will he let Heroicks chime ;
Fancy (quoth he) is loft by Rhime.
And he that's us'd to clafhing Swords
Should not delight in founds of words.
Mars with *Mercury* fhould not mingle ;
Great Warriours fhou'd fpeak big, not jingle.

Amongft this Heptarchy of Wit,
The cenfuring Age have thought it fit
To damn a Woman, 'caufe 'tis faid,
The Plays fhe vends fhe never made.
But that a *Greys Inn* Lawyer does 'em,
Who unto her was Friend in Bofom.

So

So not prefenting Scarf and Hood,
New Plays and Songs are full as good.

Thefe are the better fort I grant,
Damn'd onely by the Ignorant :
But ftill there are a fcribling Fry
Ought to be damn'd eternally ;
An unlearn'd Tribe, o'th' lower rate,
Who will be Poets fpite of Fate ;
Whofe Character's not worth reciting,
They fcarce can read, yet will be writing :
As t'other day a filly Oafe
Inftead of *Jove* did call on *Jofe :*
Whofe humble Mufe defcends to Cellars,
Or at the beft to *Herc'les Pillars.*
Now *Charon* I prefume does ftop,
Expecting one of thefe wou'd drop ;
For any fuch Poetick Damn'd-boy
Will light him home as well as Flambeau.

B 4   *Eacus*

Eacus juſt had made an end,

When did arrive the dripping Fiend,

Who did confirm the Judges ſpeech,

That *Charon* did a Light beſeech.

They fell to Conſultation grave,

To find ſome ſtrange enlightned Knave.

Faux had like t'have been the Spark,

But that his Lanthorn was too dark.

At laſt th'agreed a ſullen Quaker

Should be this buſineſs Undertaker;

The fitteſt Soul for this exploit,

Becauſe he had the neweſt Light:

Him ſoon from ſable Den they drag,

Who of his Sufferings doth brag;

And unto Heel of Fiend being ty'd,

To *Charons* Veſſel was convey'd.

Charon came home, all things were well;

This is the onely News from Hell.

As concerning Man.

TO what intent or purpose was Man made,
    Who is by Birth to misery betray'd ?
Man in his tedeous course of life runs through
More Plagues than all the Land of *Egypt* knew.
Doctors, Divines, grave Disputations, Puns,
Ill looking Citizens and scurvy Duns ;
Insipid Squires, fat Bishops, Deans and Chapters,
Enthusiasts, Prophecies, new Rants and Raptures;
Pox, Gout, Catarrhs, old Sores, Cramps, Rheums
        and Aches;
Half witted Lords, double chinn'd Bawds with
        Patches ;
Illiterate Courtiers, Chancery Suits for Life,
A teazing Whore, and a more tedeous Wife ;
Raw Inns of Court men, empty Fops, Buffoons,
Bullies robust, round Aldermen, and Clowns ;
                Gown-

Gown-men which argue, and difcufs, and prate,
And vent dull Notions of a future State;
Sure of another World, yet do not know
Whether they fhall be fav'd, or damn'd, or how.

'Twere better then that Man had never been,
Than thus to be perplex'd: *God fave the Queen.*

Have a care what you do.

I.

WHile Men endeavoured to adorn
    The guilded Creft of bloudy *Mars,*
Poor Love met with contempt and fcorn,
    Nor had he one Rag to his Arfe.

II.

His Wings were clogg'd with melting Snow,
    Hardly fupported by his Legs:

He

He had no ſtring left to his Bow,
   His Arrows too had loſt their Pegs.

III.

I who had always ſeen him gay,
   Wondered to find him thus diſtreſt ;
I told him if with me he'd ſtay,
   He might be welcom to my Breaſt.

IV.

With a faint Smile he ſhew'd his joy,
   And ſoftly to his Lodgings crept,
Where ſome deſign diſturb'd the Boy,
   He prattled all the time he ſlept.

V.

With a large Sigh his Soul I fill'd,
   Which made a rumbling in his Guts;
Into his mouth I Tears diſtill'd,
   Tears bigger far than Hazzle Nuts.

                                    His

VI.

His ſtrength return'd to every Limb,
   I let him round about me play ;
I thought my ſelf ſecure of him,
   Not dreaming he wou'd run away.

VII.

But this baſe perfidious Elf
   Ungratefully from me did part,
Not onely ſtole away himſelf,
   But took along with him my Heart.

VIII.

To *Cælia* then I did repair
   With peremptory Hue and Cry,
Being aſſur'd this ſtolen Ware
   Muſt light into her cuſtody.

e own'd it with obſequious art,
And drew on me this dire miſhap,
:ead of returning me my Heart
She gave me a confounded Clap.

A Hard Caſe.

WHen trembling Pris'ners ſtand at Bar
 In ſtrange ſuſpence about the Verdict :
nd when pronounc'd they Guilty are,
How they're aſtoniſh'd when they've heard it!

'hen in a Storm a Ship is toſs'd,
 All ask, What does the Captain ſay ?
ow they bemoan themſelves as loſt,
 When his Advice is onely, *Pray!*

And

And as it was my pleafing chance
 To meet fair *Cælia* in a Grove;
Both Time and Place confpir'd t'advance
 The innocent defigns of Love.

I thought my happinefs compleat,
 'Twas in her power to make it fo :
I ask'd her if fhe'd do the feat,
 But (filly Soul !) fhe anfwer'd, No.

Poor Pris'ners may have mercy fhewn,
 And fhipwreck'd men may have the luck
To fee their Tempefts overblown,
 But *Cælia* I fhall never

The Canary Miftrefs.

FOndling forbear, 'tis Herefie to think
There is a Miftrefs equal to thy Drink;
Or if in love with any, 't muft be rather
With that plump Girl that does call Bacchus Fa-
      ther.
Thou mayft out-look, arm'd with her warm em-
      brace,
Ten thoufand Volleys fhot from Womans Face,
Who wou'd withftand without this Aid Divine
Ten thoufand times as many Tears of thine;
As many Sighs and Prayers would be her fport,
Exalted fhe fo long maintains her Fort.
But when Diviner Sack hath fir'd thy Bloud,
Creating Flames which cannot be withftood;
To which is added Confidence as great
As his, that aim'd at Joves Celeftial Seat;

                  Boldly

Boldly march on, not granting her the leisure
Of Parly; 'tis the Speed augments the Pleasure.
If she cry out, with Kisses stop her Breath;
She cannot wish to die a better Death.
Tell her the pleasant passages between
The God of War and Loves more gentle Queen.
When feeble *Vulcan* came, and in a fear
Left they wou'd not continue longer there,
He chain'd 'em to the sport, with an intent
To keep such Lovers for a Precedent;
Glad to behold a tempting pleasure that
His weak Endeavours never could create.
Then stroke her Breasts those Mountains of De-
              light,
Whose very Touch would fire an Anchorite.
Next let thy wanton Palm a little stray,
And dip thy Fingers in the Milky Way:
Thus having raiz'd her, gently let her fall,
Loves Trumpets sound, Now Mortal have at all.

A

A happy end thus made of all your fport,
Lead her where every Lover fhou'd refort,
Where Madam *Sack*'s enthron'd, the tempting'ft
That e'er was feated in a *Venice* Glafs.   (Lafs
Laft, that this fenfe of Pleafure may remain,
Caft away Thought and fall to Drink again.
Drink off the Glaffes, fwallow every Bowl,
And pity him that fighs away his Soul
For that poor trifle Woman, who is mine
With one fmall Gallon of Immortal Wine.
To get a Miftrefs Drinking is the knack;
Love's grand exiftence is Almighty Sack.

What are you mad?

I'LL mount my thoughts to Giant height,
I'm Conftellation in conceit.
I'll pluck down *Sol*, and mount his Sphere;
Then fullen *Daphne* fhall appear,

And ſeeing me graſp *Phœbus* Rays,
Shall cringe and crown me with her Bays.
I'll rape the Moon, it ſhall be ſaid,
Cynthia hath chang'd the name of Maid ;
Her twinkling Girles ſhall all be ta'en,
No Virgin left to bear her Train.
Thus conquering Sun, Moon, and Stars,
'Gainſt Gods themſelves I'll levy Wars.
Or if on Earth my Mind can reſt,
I'll be a Monarch at the leaſt.
Our dull Plebeians ſhall grow quicker,
Rincing their muddy Brains in Liquor.
The Miſer then ſhall ſcatter Caſh,
For Wine ſhall change his Balderdaſh ;
And ſing and drink, and drink and ſing,
Till every Subject turns a King.
The conquer'd Gods ſhall make us Legs,
Intreating they may ſip the dregs.
Thus will we tipple till the World
Into Oblivion is hurld :

And when we feel old Age does come,
We'll poſt into *Elyſium* ;
And there our chiefeſt Joys ſhall be
To think of paſt Felicity.

Money's All.

BEauty is Nature's quaint Diſguiſe,
  A Covert for the Game we hunt ;
Being pinch'd but once or twice it dies,
 And leaves behind a ſlimy

Honour's the pleaſing Cheat of Men,
  The White that does diſcover Blots ;
Like to the Plague at height, which then
  Produceth gawdy purple ſpots.

Wiſdom the Souls grave penury,
  Which he that owns dares not be brave ;

But

But with dull Morals muſt comply,
    Leſt the fond Age ſhould call him Knave.

But he whoſe Wealth ne'er knew a meaſure,
    May be truly termed free ;
For while he rules alone in Treaſure,
    He commands the other three.

Several Late

S O N G S

Burlefqu'd or Varied.

As Amoret and Phyllis fate, &c.

A S *Tom* and I well warm'd with Wine
    Were fitting at the Rofe,
In came Sir *John* with dire defign
    To ply us in the clofe.

The threatning Bumpers to remove
    I whifper'd in his Ear;
Ah *Tom,* a bloudy Night 'twill prove,
    There is no ftaying here.
       There is no, &c.

          None

None ever yet had such an art
　　In filling to the Brim;
Nor can you e'er expect to part,
　　If once engag'd with him.

Fly, fly betimes, for at this rate,
　　We certainly are sunk:
In vain (said *Tom*) in vain you prate,
　　I am already drunk.
　　　　I am already drunk.

Hail to the Myrtle Shades, &c.

Pitty the private Cabal,
　　Ah pitty the Green Ribbon Club;
They've cut off poor *Strephon*'s Entail,
　　And *Strephon* has met with a rub.

Strephon has ftill the fame Greatures,
  Who fill him with many a doubt ;
But *Strephon* won't ftoop to his Betters ;
  Ah *Strephon*, ah why fo ftout !

Strephon once caper'd and pranc'd ;
  Who but *Strephon* at Masks and at Balls !
Strephon the Saraband danc'd,
  But *Strephon* now leads up the Brawls.
Strephon who ne'er had the skill
  To ufe either Figure or Trope ;
For *Strephon* has no lofty Style,
  Nor e'er was cut out for a Pope.

Strephon though not by his Tongue
  Has drawn to him Parties and Factions,
People that make the day long
  By buzzing of private Tranfactions.
Strephon has little to fay,
  But laughs at the Lord knows what ;

C 4   But

But the Club meets every day,
  And fits with eternal Chat.

The Poor Whore's Song, in allusion to
  the Begging Souldier, Good your
  Worship caft an Eye, &c.

GOod young Leacher caft an Eye
  Upon a poor Whores mifery :
Let not my antiquated Front
Make you lefs free than you were wont.
    But like a noble Rogue
    Do but difembogue,
And you fhall have our conftant vogue ;
    For I am none of thofe
    That a bulking goes,
    And often fhows
    Their Bridewell blows,

Or New Prison Lash,
For filing of Cash,
Or nimming Prigsters of their Trash.

But I at Court have often been
Within the view of King and Queen;
A Guiney to me was no more
Than Fifteen Pence to a Suburb Whore:
And when he did tilt,
I did briskly jilt,
And swallow'd *Pego* to the Hilt.
A Pox was very near,
For *Bubo* did appear,
Had not my Surgeon then been there.

Once at the Bear in *Drury Lane*
The Bullies left me for a Pawn;
But I made my party good,
To Fifteen Guinneys and a Broad.

OH

Oh you wou'd little ween
How that I have been
As great a Jilt as e'er was feen.
But if Mother *Bennet* came
With a Wheedle or a Flam,
She'd tell you how I cut the Sham.

From thence I march'd to *Crefwels* Houfe,
Under the name of a Merchants Spoufe;
And there I play'd the fecret Lover,
Left jealous Husband fhou'd difcover.
Oh then came in the Rings,
And fuch like things,
Which eldeft Prentice often brings.
But now my poor ——
Contrary to its wont,
Muft pocket any fmall Affront.

Now

Now Now the Fight's done, &c.

NOw Now the Heart's broke,
   Which fo long has complain'd ;
And *Clarinda* triumphs
   In the Conqueft fh'as gain'd.
Love laughs at the fight,
   At the mifchief does crow ;
For a Love-wounded Heart
   Is to him a fine Show.
He plays up and down, and he fports with the
         Heart,
And he fhews it about on the point of his
         Dart.

But fince the coy Nymph
   So difdainful is grown,

The power of her Charms
　　We'll for ever difown;
We'll flight the fond Brat,
　　Love no longer fhall wrack us,
We'll fhake off his Chains
　　For the pleafures of *Bacchus*.
Then fill us more Wine, fill the Glafs to the
　　　　　brim;
Thus we'll patch up our Hearts, they fhall laft
　　　　　our Life-time.

Tell me deareft pr'ythee do,
Why thou wilt and wilt not too, &c.

TEll me, *Jack*, I pr'ythee do,
　　Why the Glafs ftill fticks with you:
What does Bus'nefs fignifie,
If you let your Claret die?

Wine

Wine when firſt pour'd from the Bottle

    All its ſtrength and vigour flies;

So ſays ancient *Ariſtotle.*

        If it ſtand

        In your hand,

        It will then disband

    All its Spirits in a trice.

Who dares then refuſe to ſwallow

    All the Wine that out he puts,

Will find ſome heavy Judgments follow,

        Vinegar,

        Single Beer,

        Or ſuch diſmal Gear,

    To torment his wambling Guts.

Since to all ſubduing Wine

Lofty Arguments reſign;

He wrongs himſelf that ſits and prates

Of grave Matters or Debates.

Talk

Talk not then of Merchandizes,
　　Or what Intereſt may accrue
By Taxes, Subſidies, Exciſes,
　　　　Liberty,
　　　　Property,
　　　　Or Monopoly;
　　'Slife 'tis enough to make one ſpue.
Be as you were ever jolly,
　　Let it not ſtick at your door;
Bus'neſs is the greateſt folly.
　　　　Here's a Glaſs,
　　　　Let it paſs,
　　　　He's a formal Aſs,
　　That e'er talks of Bus'neſs more.

Mr.

Mr. Drydens *Deſcription of Night.*

ALL things were huſh'd as Nature's ſelf lay
      dead,

The Mountains ſeem to nod their drowſie
      head ;

The little Birds in Dreams their Songs re-
      peat,

And ſleeping Flowers beneath the Night dew
      ſweat.

Even Luſt and Envy ſlept, &c.

Thus Burleſqu'd.

All things were huſh as when the Drawers tread
Softly to ſteal the Key from Maſters head.

The

The dying Snuffs do twinkle in their Urns,
As if the Socket, not the Candle, burns.
The little Foot-boy fnoars upon the Stair,
And greafie Cook-maid fweats in Elbow Chair.
No Coach nor Link was heard, &c.

Difdain, yet ftill I will love thee;
Nothing, &c.

FILL't up, yet ftill I will take it ;
Fill't up, I'll ne'er forfake it :
Although
My doom I know,
This Glafs another will ufher,
Good faith it muft be fo,
Though drinking of this Brufher,
I fhall neither ftand nor go.

Now

Now at laſt the Riddle is ex-
pounded, &c.

OLD *Beelzebub* was Father of Sedition;
Pride and Arrogance began diviſion
    In Religion,
  And taught men to combine.
Fetch up the t'other double Bottle,
  I will waſh away deſign;
Bring a Spinſter, though ſhe have a hot Tail,
  No Kingdom is enflam'd by Love or Wine.

The buſie Party are the idle Fellows,
Fools that are ſuſpicious and too jealous,
    Let Hell looſe,
  The Devil's in 'em ſure.
While he that drinks *de die & in diem,*
  And all night hugs a Whore;

      D   What

What Treaſon or Rebellion can come nigh
    him,
    Since he's employ'd each minute of an hour ?

To the Tune of Per fas per nefas.

A Pox o' theſe Fellows contriving,
    They've ſpoilt our pleaſant deſign ;
We were once in a way of true living,
    Improving Diſcourſe by good Wine.
But now Converſation grows tedeous,
    O'er Coffee they ſtill confer Notes ;
'Stead of Authors both learn'd and facetious,
    They quote onely *Dugdale* and *Oats.*

A Traytor ſtill gives a denyal,
    When a Glaſs is fill'd up to the beſt :
By drinking we know who is Loyal,
    A Brimmer's the onely Teſt.

He that takes it 's untaunted of Treafon,
   He from all Impeachment is freed ;
He may lofe his Feet for a feafon,
   But never fhall lofe his Head.

An Epitaph upon the Worthy and truly Vigilant, Sam. Micoe Efq;

HEre Honeft *Micoe* lies, who never knew
   Whether the Parifh Clock went falfe or
     true.
A true bred *Englifh* Gentleman, for he
Never demanded yet *Quel heur eft il ?*
He valued not the Rife of Sun or Moon,
Nor e'er diftinguifh'd yet their Night from
     Noon.
Untill at laft by chance he clos'd his Eyes,
And Death did catch him napping by furprize.

         But

But firſt he thus ſpoke to the King of Fears,

Have I in Taverns ſpent my blooming years,

Outſate the Beadle nodding in his Chair,

Outwatch'd the Bulker and the Burglarer ;

Outdrank all meaſure fill'd above the Seal,

When ſome weak Brethren to their Beds did
    reel ;

And there when laſt nights Bottles were on
    board,

When Squires in Cloaks wrapt up in corners
    ſnoar'd ;

I onely clad in my old Night Campain,

Call'd for more Wine and drank to 'em again ?

Have I made Sir *John Robinſon* to yield,

Sent haughty *Langſton* ſtaggering from the
    Field ?

And unto meager Death now muſt I ſink,

Death that eats all without a drop of Drink ?

You ſteal my Life (grim Tyrant) 'cauſe you knew

Had I ſate up I'd kill'd more men than you.

        Quoth

Quoth furly Death, *Statutum eft, fic dico;*
Sat vigilafti——*Bonos Nochios Micoe.*

Upon Mr. Bennet, *Procurer Extra-ordinary.*

R Eader beneath this Marble Stone
Saint *Valentine*'s Adopted Son,
Bennet the Bawd now lies alone.

Here lies alone the Amorous Spark,
Who was us'd to lead them in the dark
Like Beafts by Pairs into the Ark.

If Men of Honour wou'd begin,
He'd ne'er ftick out at any Sin,
For he was ftill for Sticking't in.

If

If Justice chiefest of the Bench
Had an occasion for a Wench,
His reverend Flames 'twas he cou'd quench.

And for his Son and Heir apparent,
He cou'd perform as good an errand
Without a Tipstaff or a Warrant.

Over the Clergy had such a lock,
That he could make a Spiritual Frock
Fly off at sight of Temporal Smock.

Like *Will 'ith' wisp* still up and down
He led the Wives of *London* Town,
To lodge with Squires of high renown.

While they (poor Fools) being unaware,
Did find themselves in Mansion fair,
Near *Leic'ster Fields* or *James's Square.*

Thus

Thus Wotthy *Bennet* was imploy'd ;
At laſt he held the Door ſo wide,
He caught a cold, ſo cough'd, and dy'd.

To a late Scotch Tune.

THomas did once make my Heart full glad,
 When I ſet him up to rule at the Helm :
But *Thomas* has prov'd but a naughty Lad,
 For *Thomas* I fear has betray'd my Realm.

I gave him a Houſe, I gave him Grounds,
I gave him a hundred thouſand pounds,
I gave him the Lord knows what Gadzounds:
 But *Thomas*, &c.

The fineſt Courtier that e'er was ſeen,
He prais'd my Port, and he prais'd my Meen,

He

He prais'd all the Ladies at Court but the Q------

  Yet *Thomas, &c.*

I gave him all Chriſtian Liberty,

I let him ſometimes lig by me,

I let him feel my Ducheſſes Knee,

  Yet *Thomas, &c.*

Upon a Bowl of Punch.

THE Gods and the Goddeſſes lately did

      feaſt,

Where *Ambroſia* with exquiſite Sawces was

      dreſt.

The Edibles did with their Qualities ſuit,

But what they ſhou'd drink did occaſion diſpute.

'Twas time that old *Nectar* ſhou'd grow out of

      faſhion,

For that they have drank long before the Crea-

      tion.   When

When the Sky-coloured Cloth was drawn from
     the Board,
For the Chryſtalline Bowl Great *Jove* gave the
     word.
This was a Bowl of moſt heavenly ſize,
In which Infant Gods they did uſe to baptize.

Quoth *Jove*, We're inform'd they drink Punch
     upon Earth,
By which mortal Wights do outdo us in mirth.
Therefore our Godheads together let's lay,
And endeavour to make it much ſtronger than
     they.
'Twas ſpoke like a God, —— Fill the Bowl to
     the top,
He's caſhier'd from the Skies that leaveth one
     drop.

Apollo diſpatch'd away one of the Laſſes,
Who fetch'd him a Pitcher from Well of *Par-*
     naſſus.   To

To Poets new born this Liquor is brought,
And this they fuck in for their firft Mornings
　　　　draught.

Juno for Limons fent into her Clofet,
Which when fhe was fick fhe infus'd into
　　　　　　Poffet ;
For Goddeffes may be as fqueamifh as Gipfies,
The Sun and the Moon we find have Eclipfes.
Thefe Limons were call'd the *Hefperian* Fruit,
When vigilant Dragon was fet to look to't.
Six dozen of thefe were fqueez'd into Water,
The reft of the Ingredients in order come after.

Venus, th'Admirer of things that are fweet,
And without her Infufion there had been no
　　　　　　Treat,
Commanded two Sugar-loaves white as her
　　　　　　Doves,
Supported to th' Table by a Brace of young
　　　　Loves.　　　　　　　　So

So wonderful curious thefe Deities were,
That this Sugar they ftrain'd through a **Sieve**
of thin Air.

Bacchus gave notice by dangling a Bunch,
That without his Affiftance there could be no
Punch.
What was meant by his figns was very well
known,
So they threw in three Gallons of trufty Lan-
goon.

Mars a blunt God, who car'd not for dif-courfe,
Was feated at Table ftill twirling his Whiskers:
Quoth he, Fellow Gods and Celeftial Gall-ants,
I'd not give a Fart for your Punch without
Nants ;
Therefore Boy *Ganimede* I do command ye,
To fill up the Bowl with a Rundlet of Brandy.

Sa-

Saturn of all the Gods was the oldeſt,

And you may imagine his Stomach was coldeſt,

Did out of his Pouchet three Nutmegs pro-

duce,

Which when they were grated were put to the

Juice.

Neptune this Ocean of Liquor did crown

With a hard Sea-Biſquet well bak'd by the Sun.

The Bowl being finiſh'd, a Health was'began;

Quoth *Jove*, Let it be to our Creature call'd

Man;

'Tis to him alone theſe Pleaſures we owe,

For Heaven was never true Heaven till now.

Upon

Upon the Pyramid.

To the Tune of Packington's Pound.

I.

MY Masters and Friends, and good People
    draw near,
  For here's a new Sight which you must not
    escape,
A stately young Fabrick that cost very dear,
  Renown'd for streight body and *Barbary*
    shape ;
    A Pyramid much high'r
    Than a Steeple or Spire,
By which you may guess there has been a Fire.
  Ah *London* th'adst better have built new
    Burdellos,
  T'encourage She-Traders and lusty young
    Fellows.

II.

II.

No fooner the City had loft their old Houfes,
    But they fet up this Monument wonderfull
        tall;
Though when Chriftians were burnt, as *Fox*
        plainly fhews us,
  There was nothing fet up but his Book in
        the Hall.
      And yet thefe men can't
      In their Confcience but grant,
That a Houfe is unworthy compar'd to a Saint.
Ah London, &c.

III.

The Children of Men in erecting old *Babel,*
    To be faved from Water did onely defire:
So the City prefumes that this young one is
        able,
    When occafion fhall ferve to fecure them from
    Fire.

                  Blowing

Blowing up when all's done
Preferves beft the Town,
But this Hieroglyphick will foon be blown
down.

Ah London, &c.

IV.

Some fay it refembles a Glafs fit for Mum,
And think themfelves witty by giving Nick-
names :
An Extinguifher too 'tis fancied by fome,
As fet up on purpofe to put out the Flames.
But whatever they fhall
This Workmanfhip call,
Had it never been thought on 'thad been a
Save-all.

Ah London, &c.

V.

V.

Some Paſſengers ſeem to ſuſpect the grave
   City,
As men not ſo wiſe as they ſhou'd be, or ſo ;
And oftentimes ſay, 'Tis a great deal of pity
  So much Coin ſhould be ſpent and ſo little
    to ſhow.
   But theſe men ne'er ſtop
   To pay for going up,
For all that's worth ſeeing is when y'are atop,
 Ah London, &c.

But O you proud Nation of Citizens all,
  Suppoſing y'had rear'd but onely one ſtone,
And on it engrav'd a ſtupendious Tale,
  Of a Conflagration the like was ne'er known :
   It had been as good
   T'have humour'd the Croud,
And then y'had prevented their laughing aloud.
 Ah London, &c.

       Upon

Upon a Superannuated Couple lately married.

I.

AN Aged Couple have combin'd,
And ſtock of years together joyn'd,
To vie with Time 'tis now deſign'd.

II.

Old Emblem with thy Sythe and Sand,
Thy canker'd power they do withſtand,
Nor Fate it ſelf ſhall here command.

III.

In vain will all their Projects be ;
Great Time, they muſt acknowledge thee,
When they endeavour *Rem in Re.*

IV.

I V.

They reprefent (each tedeous night,
When they their feeble force unite)
Methufalem th'Hermaphrodite.

V.

Of the grave Poffet made with Sack
A holy Sacrament they make,
Which they with like devotion take.

V I.

The dancing Guefts like Lightning flew,
This venerable Brace mov'd too
As Cripples in the Jovial Crew.

V I I.

While Mufick play'd this folemn Pair
Kept time to every fprightly Air,
With deep-mouth'd Cough and hoarfe Catarth.

V I I I.

VIII.

And now their wishes are complete,
With chaste desires in Bed they meet;
The Wedding seems a Winding sheet.

IX.

There let us leave them, there they're safe,
The next remove is to their Grave;
Epithalamium proves their Epitaph.

On the Protestants Flail.

IN former days th' Invention was of Wracks,
To dislocate mens Joynts and break their
    Backs:
But this Protestant Flail of a severer sort is,
For *Lignum vitæ* here proves *Lignum mortis.*

The Narrative.

I.

COme prick up your Ears, if they are not
　　gone,
For this Deponent hath loft his own ;
His Neck goes next 'tis forty to one,
　　　　Which no body can deny.

I I.

Now this Deponent doth depofe,
That he was once one of the Kings Foes,
But now he thanks God he's none of thofe :
　　　　Sure our Deponent will lie.

I I I.

He fwears that once there was *Harry* the
　　Eighth,

　　　　　　　　　　　　Who

Who was divorc'd from's firſt Wife *Kate*,
And that he cut off anothers Pate,
Which no body can deny.

I V.

Even ſo (quoth he) I can witneſs bring,
That the Q——did conſent to the death of
the K——
But we are inform'd there was no ſuch thing;
For our Deponent will lie.

V.

He ſwears that before the Tower of *Babel*
Kain knock'd out the Brains of his Brother
Abel ;
Here he ſwears to a Truth and not to a Fable ;
Which no body can deny.

V I.

Ev en ſo (quoth he) ſome bloudy work

E 3 Was

Was carried on by his Brother of *Y*——

But His Highnefs is neither a *Jew* nor a *Turk*,

For our Deponent will lie.

VII.

He fwears that once in *Noah*'s time,

There was a great Floud that brought a great

Stream,

And all were drown'd that cou'd not fwim;

Which no body can deny.

VIII.

And now (God blefs us) we're all in a fright,

For we had like t'have been ruin'd quite,

Our Throats fhould all have been cut in the

night;

But our Deponent will lie.

IX.

Further he fwears that S. *Peter* from Heav'n,

H

Had such an absolute power given,

That whom he pleas'd were condemn'd or for-

given,

Which no body can deny.

X.

Even so (saith he) Commissions went out

From the Pope to raise both Horse and Foot,

That whom he pleas'd he might slash and cut;

But our Deponent will lie.

X I.

Some where or other S. *Paul* does aver,

That an Oath puts an end to all bustle and stir,

By which he confirms it is lawful to swear;

Which no body can deny.

X I I.

There was foolish swearing in former days,

But

But our Deponent has alter'd the cafe,
For 'has made more mifchief than ever there
      was,
          For our Deponent will lie.

The fourteenth Ode *of the fecond Book*
of Horace.

Eheu fugaces, Pofthume, Pofthume,
Labuntur anni——

SEE, *Pofthumus*, how years do fly;
Nor can the fmootheft Piety
    Fill up one wrinkle in the Face,
    Or ftop Old Ages certain pace,
        Or quell Mortality.

When dying if thou fhouldft defign
To offer up at *Pluto*'s Shrine,

                                A

As many Bullocks fat and fair,

As th'are days in every year,

One hour would not be thine.

See the thrice bulky *Geryon* ftand,

Shackled in Ropes of *Stygian* :

On t'other fide the doleful Pool

See the extended *Tityus* roul,

Where all Mankind muft land.

This irkfom Shore muft entertain

The greateft Prince that e'er fhall reign:

As great a welcom fhall be there

Made to the meaneft Cottager;

Diftinctions are in vain.

In vain we fhun the chance of War,

Where the moft frequent dangers are.

In

In vain we do fecure our felves
From troubled Seas, or Sands, or Shelves,
　　　Or a cold Winter fear.

By all the Human Race at laft
Muddy *Cocytus* muft be paft;
　　Where th'impious Daughters fill a Sieve,
　　Where Sifyphus in vain does ftrive
　　　　To ftick the Rowler faft.

We bid Farwell to Land and Houfe,
To th' joys of an untainted Spoufe;
　　And to the filent Groves and Trees,
　　Whofe Height and Shade at once do pleafe :
　　　　But there fad Cyprefs grows.

Then fhall rich Wines brought from *Campain*,
Which you with Locks and Bolts detain,

Be by your worthy Heir let loofe,
To give a Tincture round the Houfe,
   Where he does entertain.

The tenth Ode of the fecond Book of Horace.

Rectiùs vives, Licine, neque altum
Semper urgendo———

THat thou mayft fteer thy courfe with great-
     er eafe,
Plunge not far amidft the deepeft Seas:
Or fill'd with horror when the Ocean roars,
Prefs not hard upon unequal Shores.
   Who ever does admire the Golden Mean,
Is not pent up in Cottages unclean;
Inhabits not obfcure and fordid Cells,
Nor courts the lofty Hall where Envy dwells.

The

The Pine Tree's vex'd by winds becaufe
'tis tall ;
The higher the Tower, the greater is its fall.
By Heavens Artillery are Mountains fhook,
And mightieft Hills are fooneft Thunder
ftrook.

In adverfe Times a well prepared Mind
With reafon hopes a better change to find;
In profp'rous days wifhes no further good,
But modeftly does fear Viciffitude.
Heaven doth disfigure Earth with Winters
Rain,
And the fame Heaven guilds the Earth again.
If at one inftant things fucceed not well,
There follows not an everlafting Ill.
From Bow and Dart *Apollo* doth retire,
And fometimes takes in hand his charming Lyre,
And by foft Notes excites the Female Quire.
When in fome dangerous Straits your Barque
fhall ride,

Let

Let never failing Courage be your Guide :
But if your Fortune blow aufpicious Gales,
Let Wifdom then contract your ftrutting Sails.

Horace's *well wifhes to a fcurvy Poet gone to Sea,* Epode 10. in Mævium.

Mala foluta navis exit alite,
Ferens olentem Mævium, &c.

Wlth an unhappy Freight that Ship is
     ftor'd,
That took the fulfom *Mævius* aboard.
Aufter remember what you have to do,
'Tis in your power to fplit the Ship in two.
Eurus the Black, this your Command fhall be,
To fpoil the Tackle, and difturb the Sea.

Aquilo

Aquilo rife, and be your Fury fhown,

As much as when you Trees have overthrown.

And in dark night no friendly Star appear,

As when *Orion* leaves the Hemifphere.

Nor more of Calm at Sea let him enjoy,

Than conquering *Grecians* when they fail'd

from *Troy*;

When *Pallas* to avenge the fin of Fire,

By water made *Ajax*'s Crew expire.

What fport'twoud be t'obferve the Sailers fweat;

And fee thy Earthen Face look paler yet !

To hear thy Howlings and unmanly Cries,

In vain befeeching angry Deities !

Or let the Southern Winds drive thee away

Into the bellowing Gulph of *Adria*.

But if thy Carcafe fhould be caft on fhore,

That Cormorants the Carrion may devour :

To th'Tempefts then a Holyday we'll keep,

By offering up a Ram or fome black Sheep.

A Call

A Call to the Guard by a Drum.

RAt too, rat too, rat too, rat tat too, tat
   rat too,
With your Nofes all fcabb'd and your Eyes
   black and blew,
All ye hungry poor Sinners that Foot Souldiers
   are,
Though with very fmall Coyn, yet with very
   much Care,
From your Quarters and Garrets make hafte to
   repair,
     To the Guard, to the Guard.

From your forry Straw Beds and bonny white
   Fleas,
From your Dreams of Small Drink and your
   very fmall eafe,
From your plenty of ftink, and no plenty of
   room,
From your Walls daub'd with Phlegm fticking
   on 'em like Gum,
And Ceiling hung with Cobwebs to ftanch a
   cut Thumb,
     To the Guard, &c.

From

From your crack'd Earthen Pifpots where no
    Pifs can ftay,
From Roofs bewrit with Snuffs in Letters the
    wrong way ;
From one old broken Stool with one unbroken
    Leg,
One Box with ne'er a Lid to keep ne'er a Rag,
And Windows that of Storms more than your
    felves can brag,
          To the Guard, &c.

With trufty Pike and Gun, and the other rufty
    Tool ;
With Heads extremely hot, and with Hearts
    wondrous cool ;
With Stomachs meaning none (but Cooks and
    Sutlers) hurt ;
With two old totter'd Shooes that difgrace the
    Town Dirt ;
With forty fhreds of Breeches, and no one fhred
    of Shirt,
          To the Guard, &c.

See they come, fee they come, fee they come, fee
    they come,
With Allarms in their Pates to the eall of a Drum ;
Some lodging with Bawds (whom the modeft
    call Bitches)
With their Bones dry'd to Kexes, and Legs fhrunk
    to Switches ;
                With

With the Plague in the Purse, and the Pox in the
          Breeches,
             To the Guard, &c.

Some from snoring and farting, and spewing on
          Benches,
Some from damn'd fulsom Ale, and more damn'd
          fulsom Wenches;
Some from Put, and Size Ace, and Old Sim, this
          way stalk;
Each mans Reeling's his gate, and his Hickup his
          talk,
With two new Cheeks of Red from ten old
          Rows of Chalk,
             To the Guard, &c.

Here come others from scuffling, and damning
          mine Host,
With their Tongues at last tam'd, but with Faces
          that boast
Of some Scars by the Jordan, or Warlike Quart
          Pot,
For their building of Sconces and Volleys of Shot,
Which they charg'd to the mouth, but discharg'd
          ne'er a Groat,
             To the Guard, &c.

They for Valour in black too, the Chaplain does
          come!
From his preaching o'er Pots now to pray o'er a
          Drum.   F   All
)

All ye whoring and ſwearing old Red Coats
                draw near,
Like to Saints in Red Letters liſten and give ear,
And be godly awhile ho, and then as you were,
                To the Guard, &c.

After ſome canting terms, To your Arms, and the
                like,
Such as Poyſing your Muſquet, or Porting your
                Pike ;
To the right, To the left, or elſe Face about ;
After ratling your Sticks, and your ſhaking a
                Clout,
Haſt your Infantry Troops that mount the Guard
                on foot,
                To the Guard, &c.

Captain *Hector* firſt marches, but not he of *Troy*,
But a Trifle made up of a Man and a Boy ;
See the Man ſcant of Arms in a Scarf does
                abound,
Which preſages ſome ſwaggering, but no bloud
                nor wound ;
Like a Rainbow that ſhews the World ſhan't be
                drown'd ;
                To the Guard, &c.

As the Tinker wears Rags whileſt the Dog bears
                the Budget,
So the Man ſtalks with Staff whileſt the Footboy
                does trudge it   With

                                                6

Vith the Tool he ſhould work with (that's Half
     Pike you'll ſay ;)
But what Captain's ſo ſtrong his own Arms to
     convey,
When he marches o'er loaden with ten other
     mens Pay?
          To the Guard, &c.

n his March (if you mark) he's attended at leaſt
With Stinks ſixteen deep, and about five abreaſt,
Made of Ale and Mundungus, Snuff, Rags, and
     brown Cruſt for,
While he wants twenty Taylors to make up the
     cluſter,
Which declares that his Journey's not now to the
     Muſter,
          But to the Guard, &c.

Some with Muſquet and Belly uncharg'd march
     away,
With Pipes black as their Mouths, and ſhort as
     their Pay ;
Whileſt their Coats made of holes ſhew like
     Bone-lace about 'em,
And their Bandeliers hang like to Bobbins with-
     out 'em,
And whileſt Horſemen do cloath 'em, theſe Foot-
     ſcrubs do clout 'em,
          For the Guard, &c.

Some with Hat ty'd on one fide, and Wit ty'd
    neither;
Wear gray Coats and gray Cattle, fee their Wei
    ches run hither,
For to peep through Red Lettice and dark Ce
    lar doors,
To behold 'em wear Pikes rufty juft like their
    Whores,
As flender as their Meals and as long as their
    Scores,
        To the Guard, &c.

Some with Tweedle, wheedle, wheede; whileft
    we beat Dub a Dub;
Keep the bafe *Scotifh* noife, and as bafe *Scotifh*
    fcrub:
Then with Body contracted, a Rag open fpread,
Comes a thing with red Colours, and Nofe full
    as red;
Like an Enfign to the King, and to the Kings
    Head,
        Towards the Guard, &c.

Two Commanders come laft, the Lieutenant pei
    haps,
Full of Low Country Stories and Low Country
    Claps.
To be next him the other takes care not to fail,
Powder Monkey by name that vents ftink by
    whole fale,

'or where fhould the Fart be but juft with the
   Tail
    Of the Guard ? &c.

\nd now hey for the King Boys, and hey for the
   Court,
Vhich is guarded by thefe as the Tower is by
   Dirt;
Thefe *Whitehall* muft admit and fuch other un-
   houfe ye,
\ach day lets in the drunk, whilft it lets out the
   drowfie,
\nd no place in the world fhifts fo oft to be lowfie.

   Thank the Guard, &c.

ome to *Scotland-Yard* fneak, and the Sutlers wife
   kiffes ;
\ut defpairing of Drink till fome Countryman
   piffes,
\nd pays too (for no place in the Court muft be
   given)
'o the Can-office then, all a *Foot-Soldier's* Heav'n,
Vhere he finds a foul *Fox*, foon, and cures Sir----

   On the Guard, &c.

ome at Sh---houfe publick(where a Rag always
   goes)

          At

At once empty their Guts and diminish their
       Clothes.
Though their Mouths are poor Pimps (Whore
      and Bacon being all
Their chief Food) yet their Bums we true Cour-
      tiers may call,
For what they eat in the Suburbs, they sh——
      at *Whitehall*,
         For the Guard, &c.

Such a like Pack of Cards to the *Park* making
      entry,
Here and there deal an Ace, which the *Jews* call
      a Centry,
Which in bad Houses of Boards stand to tell
      what a clock 'tis,
Where they keep up tame Redcoats as men keep
      up tame Foxes,
Or Apothecaries lay up their Dogs Turds in
      Boxes.
         Oh the Guard, &c.

Some of these are planted (though it has been
      their lucks
Oft to steal Country Geese) now to watch the
      Kings Ducks ;
While some others are set in the side that has
      Wood in,
To stand Pimps to black Masques that are oft
      thither footing,
               Just

Juſt as Houſewives ſet Cuckolds to ſtir their
   Black Pudding.
     Oh the Guard, &c.

Whileſt another true *Trojan* to ſome paſſage runs,
As to keep in the Debtors, ſo to keep out the
   Duns ;
Or a Prentice, or his Miſtreſs, with Oaths to
   confound,
Till he hyes him from the Park as from forbid-
   den ground,
'Cauſe his Credit is whole, and his Wench may
   be ſound,
     And quits the Guard, &c.

Now it's night, and the Patrole in Alehouſe
   drown'd,
For nought elſe but the Pot and their Brains
   walk the round ;
Whileſt like Hell the Commanders Guard-cham-
   ber does ſhew,
There's ſuch damning themſelves and all elſe of
   the Crew,
For though theſe cheat the Men, they give the
   Devil his due,
     On the Guard, &c.

Whileſt a Main after Main at old Hazard they
   throw,
And their Quarrels grow high as their Money
   grows low ; F 4   Strait

Strait they threaten hard (ufing bad Faces for
        Frowns)
To revenge on the Flefh, the default of the
        Bones,
But the Blood's in their Hofe, and in Oaths all
        their Wounds.

Like the Guard, &c.

In the Morning they fight, juft as much as they
        pray ;
For fome one to the King does the Tidings con-
        vey
For preventing of *Murder* ; Oh 'tis a wife
        way !
Though not one of 'em knows (as a thoufand
        dare fay)
That belongs to a dead man, unlefs in his
        pay

For the Guard, &c.

With their Skins they march home no more hurt
        than their Drums,
But for fcratching of Faces, or biting of
        Thumbs ;
And now hey for fat *Alewives,* and *Tradefmen*
        grown lean ;
For the Captain grown *Bankrupt,* recruits him
        again,

                            With

With fending out Tickets, and turning out
  Men
    From the Guard, &c.

Strait the poor Rogue's cafhier'd with a Cane,
  and a Curfe,
Fall from wounding no Men, now to cut ev'ry
  Purfe :
And what then? Man's a *Worm*; thefe we Glow-
  worms may name :
For as they'r dark of Body, have Tails all of
  flame.
So tho' thofe liv'd in Oaths, yet they die with
  a *Pfalm.*

    Farewell Guard, &c.

Dr.

Dr. Wild's *Humble Thanks for His Majesty's gracious Declaration for Liberty of Conscience*, Mar. 15. 72.

NO not one word can I of this great deed
In *Merlin* or old Mother *Shipton* read!
Old *Tyburn* take thofe *Tychobrahe* Imps,
As *Silger*, who would be accounted Pimps
To the Amorous Planets; they the Minute know
When *Jove* did Cuckold old *Amphytrio*,
Ken *Mars*, and made *Venus* wink, and glances
Their clofe Conjunctions and Midnight Dances;
When coftive *Saturn* goes to ftool, and vile
Thief *Mercury* doth pick his Fob the while;
When Lady *Luna* leaks, and makes her Man
Throw't out of Window into th'Ocean.
More fubtil than th'Excifemen here below,
What's fpent in every Sign in Heaven they know.

Cunning

Cunning Intelligencers, they will not mifs
To tell us next year the fuccefs of this;
They correfpond with *Dutch* and *Englifh* Star,
As one once did with C H A R L E S and *Oliver*.
The *Bankers* alfo might have (had they gone)
What Planet govern'd the Exchequer known.
Old *Lilly*, though he did not love to make
Any words on't, faw the *Englifh* take
Five of the *Smyrna* Fleet, and if the Sign
Had been *Aquarius*, then they'd made them Nine.
When *Sagittarius* took his aim to fhoot
At Bifhop *Cofin*, he fpied him no doubt;
And with fuch force the winged Arrow flew,
Inftead of one Church Stag he killed two;
Glocefter and *Durham* when he efpy'd,
Let Lean and Fat go together he cry'd:
Well *Wille Lilly*, thou knew'ft all this as well
As I, and yet wouldft not their Lordfhips tell.
I know thy Plea too, and muft it allow,
Prelats fhould know as much of Heaven as thou.

But

But now, Friend *William*, fince it's done and paft,
Pray thee give us *Phanaticks* but one caft,
What thou forefawft of *March* the Fifteenth laft ⁵
When fwift and fudden as the Angels fly,
Th' Declaration for Confcience Liberty ;
When things of Heaven burft from the Royal
More fragrant than the Spices of the Eaft. (Breft ⁵
I know in next years Almanack thou'lt write,
Thou fawft the King and Council over night,
Before that morn, al! fit in Heaven as plain
To be difcern'd, as if 'twere *Charles's Wain*.
Great *B*, great *L*, and two great *A A's* were chief,
Under great *Charles* to give poor *Fan's* relief.
Thou fawft Lord *Arlington* ordain the Man
To be the firft Lay-Metropolytan.
Thou fawft him give Induction to a *Spittle*,
And conftitute our Brother *Tom Dolittle*.
In the *Bears* Paw, and the *Bulls* right Eye,
Some detriment to Priefts thou didft efpy ;

And

And though by *Sol in Libra* thou didſt know
Which way the Scale of Policy would go;
Yet *Mercury in Aries* did decree,
That *Wooll* and *Lamb* ſhould ſtill Conformiſts be.
But hark you *Will*, Steer-poching is not fair;
Had you amongſt the Steers found this *March-hare*,
Bred of that luſty Puſs the Good Old Cauſe,
Religion reſcued from Informing Laws;
You ſhould have yelp'd aloud, Hanging's the end,
By Huntſmens rule, of Hounds that will not ſpend.
Be gone thou and thy canting Tribe, be gone;
Go tell thy deſtiny to followers none:
Kings Hearts and Councils are too deep for thee,
And for thy Stars and *Dæmons* ſcrutiny.
King *Charles* Return was much above thy skill
To fumble out, as 'twas againſt thy will.
From him who can the Hearts of Kings inſpire,
Not from the Planets, came that ſacred Fire
Of Sovereign Love, which broke into a flame;
From God and from his King alone it came.

To

To the King.

So great, fo univerfal, and fo free !
This was too much, great *Charles*, except for thee,
For any King to give a Subject hope :
To do thus like thee would undo the Pope.
Yea tho his Vaffals fhould their wealth combine,
To buy Indulgence half fo large as thine ;
No, if they fhould not onely kifs his Toe,
But *Clements podex*, he'd not let them go:
Whileft thou to's fhame, thy immortal glory,
Haft freed *All Souls* from real Purgatory ;
And given *All Saints* in Heaven new joys, to fee
Their Friends in *England* keep a Jubilee.
Sufpect them not, Great Sir, nor think the worft;
For fudden Joys like Grief confound at firft.
The fplendor of your Favour was fo bright,
That yet it dazles and o'erwhelms our fight:
Drunk with her cups my Mufe did nothing mind,
And untill now her Feet fhe could not find.

Gree-

Greedinefs makes prophannefs i'th'firft place;

Hungry men fill their bellies, then fay Grace.

We wou'd have Bonfires, but that we do fear

The name of *Incend'ary* we may hear :

We wou'd have Mufick too, but 'twill not do,

For all the Fidlers are *Conformifts* too :

Nor can we ring, the angry Churchman fwears

By the Kings leave the Bells and Ropes are theirs;

And let 'em take 'em, for our Tongues fhall fing

Your Honour louder than their Clappers ring.

Nay, if they will not at this Grace repine,   (wine.

We'll drefs the Vineyard, they fhall drink the

Their Church fhall be the Mother, ours the Nurfe;

Peter fhall preach, *Judas* fhall bear the purfe.

No *Bifhops*, *Parfons*, *Vicars*, *Curates*, we

But onely *Minifters* defire to be.

We'll preach in Sackcloth, they fhall read in Silk;

We'll feed the Flock, and let them take the Milk.

Let but the *Blackbirds* fing in Bufhes cold,

And may the *Jackdaws* ftill the Steeples hold.

We'll

We'll be the *Feet*, the *Back*, and *Hands*, and they
Shall be the *Belly*, and devour the prey.
The Tythe-pig shall be theirs, we'll turn the Spit;
We'll bear the *Cross*, they onely *sign* with it.
But if the Patriarchs shall envy show
To see their younger Brother *Joseph* go
In Coat of divers colours, and shall fall
To rend it 'cause it's not Canonical;
Then may they find him turn a Dreamer too,
And live themselves to see his Dream come true.
May rather they and we together joyn
In all what each can; but they have the Coyn;
With *prayers and tears* such Service much avail;
With *tears* to swell your *Seas*, with *prayers* your
   Sails;
And with Men too from both our Parties; such
I'm sure we have can cheat or beat the *Dutch*.
A thousand *Quakers*, Sir, our side can spare;
Nay two or three, for they great Breeders are.
The Church can match us too with Jovial Sirs,
Informers, *Singingmen*, and *Paraters*.
Let the King try, set these upon the Decks
Together, they will *Dutch* or *Devil* vex.
Their Breath will mischief further than a Gun,
And if you lose them you'll not be undone.
Pardon, Dread Sir, nay pardon this course Paper,
Your Licenfe 'twas made this poor Poet caper.

ITER BOREALE.

These

These for his Old Friend Doctor
Wild, *Author of the* Humble
Thanks, &c.

SIR,

HAD I believ'd report, that said
    These Rhymes by Doctor *Wild* were made,
I long before this time had sent
Some symptoms of our discontent.
For since y' have left off being witty,
Your *humble thanks* deserves our pitty.

   I can't imagine what you'l do,
Your Muse turn'd *Non-conformist* too ?
And will not easily dispence
With the old way of writing sence !
She hath receiv'd, if that be true,
As much *Indulgence* then as you.

G

Surely

Surely (*Dear Sir*) you did not pray
Since you convers'd with *Tycho Brah.*
Jove play'd the wag, and *Luna* pift,
Do thefe things with *Free-Grace* confift?

Celeftial Signs ferve to exprefs
The good man's heav'nly mindednefs;
There are but Twelve of them in Heaven,
Yet he'll name one by one eleven;
And if you're not in too much haft,
'Tis ten to one, he names the laft.

You had been horribly put to't,
If *Sagittarius* could not fhoot:
Aquarius and the *Smyrna* Fleet,
I'll fwear, a very good conceit.

But, Doctor, let us know, why will ye
Thus vex your felf at *William Lilly?*
'Tis true, he could not find it out,
That *March* would bring all this about;

But

But on that day you well might gather
That there would be some change of weather :
And change of weather in a Nation
Portends a kind of alteration.

   This favour, you do say, did come
Fragrant and full of all perfume,
Like Eaſtern Spices (it ſhould ſeem)
This had done rarely in a Theme.
To the next Column ----- let us ſee
How you diſcourſe His MAJESTY.
Where every ſolemn Epithite
Does look like Grace before you eat,
Which being ſaid, as rudely you
Do take the Boldneſs to fall to,
With Rhymes moſt reverently ſent
About *Pope Clement*'s Fundament,
And *Puns* that would provoke the hate
Of any under Graduate.

           G 2   *Peter*

Peter Non-con (it feems) muft pray,
And *Judas* Church muft take the Pay.
Some angry men would call him rude Afs,
That calls the Church of *England Judas*,
You'l be no *Bifhop*, nor no *Curate*,
'Tis only Minifter that you 're at.
Minifter ! It founds, methinks,
Like Paftor *Clark* of *Bennet Fynks*.

  Thefe Favours which the King doth heap
Upon your Head, hath made you *leap*.
And fince y' have found your feet again,
The *Gout*'s got up into your *Brain* :
If *cap'ring* be fo fine a thing,
Pr'ythee come over for the King.

Your humble Servant,

O B E D I A H.

Ill Painters when they make a Sign
Either of Talbot or of Swine,
To satisfie all Persons rogant,
That they might make a Hog or Dog on't;
Do never think it any shame
To underwrite the Creature's Name.
WILD *made some Verses you must know,*
ITER BOREALE *is below.*

——————— ———————

THE

R A M B L E.

WHile Duns were knocking at my Door,
I lay in Bed with recking Whore,
With Back so weak and P---- so sore,
        You'd wonder,

I rouz'd my Doe, and lac'd her Gown,
I pin'd her Whisk, and drop't a Crown,
She pift, and then I drove her down,
> Like Thunder.

From Chamber then I went to dinner,
I drank fmall Beer like mournful Sinner,
And ftill I thought the Devil in her
> *Clitoris*,

I fate at *Muskats* in the dark,
I heard a Tradef-man and a Spark,
An Atturney and a Lawyer's Clark,
> Tell Stories.

From thence I went, with muffled Face,
To the Duke's Houfe, and took a place,
In which I fpu'd, may't pleafe his Grace,
> Or Highnefs ;

> Shou'd

Shou'd I been hang'd I could not chufe
But laugh at Whores that drop from Stews,
Seeing that Miſtris *Marg'ret* -------
                              So fine is.

When Play was done, *I* call'd a Link,
I heard ſome paltry pieces chink
Within my Pockets, how d' ee think
                              I' employ'd 'em?

Why, *S*ir, I went to Miſtriſs *Spering*,
Where ſome were curſing, others ſwearing,
Never a Barrel better Herring,
                              per ſidem,

Seven's the main, 'tis Eight, God dam 'me,
'Twas ſix, ſaid I, as God ſhall ſa' me,
Now being true you cou'd not blame me
                              ſo ſaying,

Sa' me! quoth one, what Shamaroon
Is this, has begg'd an Afternoon
Of's Mother, to go up and down
     A playing?

This was as bad to me as killing,
Miſtake not Sir, ſaid I, I'm willing,
And able both, to drop a ſhilling,
     Or two Sir:

Goda'mercy then, ſaid Bully *Hec*----
With Whiſkers ſtern, and Cordubeck
Pinn'd up behind, his ſcabby Neck
     To ſhew Sir.

With mangled fiſt he graſp'd the Box,
Giving the Table bloody knocks,
He throws ---- and calls for Plague and Pox
     T' aſſiſt him;

       Some

Some twenty fhillings he did catch,
H'ad like t'have made a quick difpatch,
Nor could, Time's Regifter, my Watch
    Have mift him.

As Luck would have it, in came *Will*,
Perceiving things went very ill,
Quoth he, y' ad better go and fwill
    Canary,

We fteer'd our courfe to *Dragon Green*,
Which is in *Fleetftreet* to be feen,
Where we drank Wine---not foul---but clean
    contrary.

Our Hoft, y'cleped *Thomas Hammond*,
Prefented flice of Bacon Gammon,
Which made us fwallow Sack as Salmon
    Drink water,
      Which

Being o'er-warm'd with laſt debauch,
I grew as drunk as any Roch,
When hot-bak'd-Wardens did approach,

        Or later,

We broke the Glaſſes out of hand,
As many Oaths I'd at command
As *Haſtings, Sabin, Sunderland,*

        Or *Ogle,*

Then I cry'd up *Sir Henry Vane,*
And ſwore by God I would maintain
Epiſcopacy was too plain

        A juggle.

But oh! the damn'd confounded Fate
Attends on drinking Wine ſo late,
I drew my Sword on honeſt *Kate*

        O'th' Kitchin,

        Which

Which *H*-----'s Wife would not endure,
I told her tho' fhe look'd demure,
She came but lately I was fure

    From Bitching.

A Club there was in t'other Room,
I bolted in, being known to fome,
Such men are not in Chriftendom

    For jefting,

They ufe a plain familiar ftile,
Appearing friendly all the while,
Yet never part without a Broil

    Inteftin.

The firft as Steward did appear,
A ftrange conceited Barrifter,
Who on all Matters will infer

    His Reading,

      A

A Band 'had on, that's very plain,
A Velvet Coat, a ſhining Cane,
Some Law, leſs Wit, and not a grain
                              Of Breeding.

The Company were in a fit
Of talking News about *Maeſtricht,*
How that the Prince's leaving it
                              Was ſudden,

Quoth he, (becauſe they ſhould ſay
That he knew leſs of this than they)
Juſt ſuch a caſe I read this day
                              In *Plowden.*

An angry Captain that was there,
Could Indignation not forbear,
'Zounds, ſayes he, did Man e're hear
                              Such Non-ſence ?

                                        We

We talk of Sieges, Camps, and Forts,
This Fool's a keeping Country Courts,
With musty Law and dull Reports,

        Damn'd long since,

Go bolt your Cafes at the Fire,
From *Plowden*, *Perkins*, *Raftal*, *Dyer*,
Such heavy stuff does rather tire

        Than please us :

Tell not us of Iffue Male,
Of Simple Fee, and Special Tail,
Of Feofments, Judgments, Bills of Sale,

        And Leafes.

Can you difcourfe of Hand-Granadoes,
Of Sally-Ports and Ambufcadoes,
Of Counterfcarps and Pallizadoes,

        And Trenches,

           Of

Of Baſtions, blowing up of Mines,
Or of Communication Lines,
Or can you gueſs the great Deſigns
               The *French* has ?

The Barriſter began to ſtart
To hear ſuch bloody terms of Art,
And did deſire with all his heart
               A Farewel;

Till younger Member of the Houſe,
Reſenting this as an Abuſe,
Thought it convenient to eſpouſe
               His Quarrel.

This was a ſpruce young Squire that
Knew the true Manage of the Hat,
And every morning ty'd Cravat
               With Project :

                    One

One that was fure he knew the Town,
To men of Fringe and Feather known,
'Mongft whom all Law he wou'd difown,
> And Logick.

Captain, quoth he, I'll tell you thus:
You are miftaken much in us,
With dint of Sword we can difcufs;
> 'Tis true Sir,

You trail'd a Pike, or fome fuch thing,
In *Holland*, here you huff and ding:
And all the Town (forfooth) muft ring
> Of you, Sir.

I can remember you at *Lambs*,
Whither you'd come with forty fhams;
And fwore you wou'd renounce all Games
> But Tennis:

> Laft

Laſt night (ſuch luck ne'r man had yet)
You play'd with Counteſs at Picquet,
And that ſhe did (by Jeſus) get
      Twelve Guinnies ;

Nay worſe --- juſt parting with my Lord,
He fancy'd much your Silver Sword,
And you wear his not worth a Turd ----
      --- A Bawble;

But for the Hilt he's like to pay,
For you will have his Iron Grey :
A ſwifter Nag is not this day
      In ſtable.

And all the great deſign of this
Is but to borrow half a Piece,
Or be excuſ'd (if Ready miſs)
      From Clubbing:

         The

The Captain ſwell'd, yet did not know
Whether the Youth would fight or no,
Or if 'twere ſafe to give the Foe

       A drubbing.

Company's here, and for their ſake,
Quoth he, ſome other time I'll take,
For I did never love to make

       A Buſtle,

Even when you pleaſe, quoth Younker, then
I'm every Evening to be ſeen
'Mongſt witty Coffee-drinkers in

       Street *Ruſſel.*

One that was Doctor, Rook, and Quack,
With whom the Captain us'd to ſnack,
Becauſe he'd make the firſt attack

       On Bubble.

      H   D

Did think it fit to do him right,
Altho' he knew he would not fight,
Yet Cully he would fore affright
                And trouble.

Therefore the Captain's part he took;
Home Lad, quoth he, unto your Book,
If Letters fail, Go Bully-rock
                The Carrier,

For here you muft not vent your ftuff,
We underftand you well enough:
You muft not think to rant and huff
                A Warrier.

I knew when *Animal* and *Ens*
Was once the chief of your pretence,
But now you think y'ave fprucer Senfe
                And Knowledge.

                    When

When firſt this Town y'arriv'd unto,
The only Bu'sneſs y' ad to do
Was to enquire out thoſe that knew

      Your Colledge.

Certainly Mortal never ſaw
A thing ſo pert, ſo dull, ſo raw,
And yet 'twou'd put a Caſe in Law,

      If they wou'd,

Then it began to viſit Playes,
And on the Women it wou'd gaze,
And looked like Love in a Maze,

      Or a Wood.

Into Fop-corner you wou'd get,
And uſe a ſtrange obſtreperous Wit,
Not any quiet to the Pit

      Allowing :

    H 2   And

And when my Lord came in, you'd ſpy,
If toward you he caſt an Eye,
Y' had lucky opportunity
     Of bowing,

At laſt you got a ſwinging Clap,
Which ran upon you like a Tap,
And lay for Cure of this miſhap
     At *Tooting,*

Then you writ Letters of Advice
To Parent, for ſome freſh ſupplies,
Pretending to the exerciſe
     Of Mooting :

At length you underſtood a Dye,
Carry'ing in Fob variety
Of Goads, of Bars, of Flats, of High
     And Low-Dyce.

       But

But when you hear the fatal doom,

That Father ſhall remand you home,

It hardly will appear you come

                        From Studies.

The Youth was juſt a throwing Glaſs

Of Wine into the Doctor's Face,

When Barriſter took Heart of Grace,

                        And courage:

Doctor, ſayes he, you are a Cheat,

A greater Knave walks not the Street,

A verrier Quack one ſhall not meet

                        In our Age.

Doctors of Phyſick we indeed

Do moſt abominably need :

If you are one, that ſcarce can read

                        A Ballat,

You ferv'd a Doctor, --- true, from whom
You ftole Receipts, being his Groom,
Or waiting on him in his Room,

     As Valet,

On Serving-men you us'd to cut,
Giving 'em the high Game at Put,
And made the Fellows ftill run out

     Their wages,

With Chamberlain you quit old fcores,
Ruin the Tapfter at all Fours,
And ftill obferve the Carriers hours,

     And Stages.

T' Apothecary next you go,
To whom your ftollen Receipts you fhow,
That y'ave no Learning he does know,

     And fmall Parts:

         Yet

Yet for Advantage does proclaim

You as the eldest Son of Fame,

And swears your Cures have got a Name

            In all Parts.

Then take your Lodgings at his House,

With care and secrecy to chouse

Those Fools incurable, that thus

            Are minded,

If y'are defir'd to write a Bill,

Your Eyes have a defluxion still,

That if you do but touch a Quill,

            You're blinded.

'Mongſt gilded Books on ſhelves you ſqueeze

Old *Gallen* and *Hippocrates,*

For ſuch learn'd men (ſay you) as theſe

            I'll ſtickle.

Tho' what they were you cannot tell,
Giants they might have been as well,
Or two Arch-Angels, *Gabriel*,

> And *Mich'el*.

In short, you are an empty Sawse ----
Before this word quite out he draws,
The Doctor struck him crofs the Jaws,

> God blefs us !

The Student then propos'd a flap,
Which on Quack's beft of Eyes did hap,
With might and main-- on Youth fell Cap---

> ---tain *Beffus*.

I'th' Room was Juftice *Middlefex*,
Who underftanding Statute *Lex*,
Being unwilling to perplex

> A Riot,

> Softly

Softly as he could fpeak, did cry,
(Which no Body obferv'd but I)
My Friends, in Name of Majefty,

     Be quiet.

The Youngfter firft defir'd a Truce,
Becaufe Cravat from Neck hung loofe,
Captain, quoth he, your Weapon choofe,

     I'll fight 'ee:

Nay then, thought I, if fo it be,
You're very likely to agree,
There's no Diverfion more for me,

     Good night t'ee.

And having now difcharg'd the Houfe,
We did referve a gentle Soufe,
With which we drank another roufe

     At the Bar :

       And

And good Chriftians all attend,
To Drunkennefs pray put an end,
I do advife you as a Friend,
                    And Neighbour.

For lo ! that Mortal here behold,
Who cautious was in dayes of old,
Is now become rafh, fturdy, bold,
                    And free Sir ;

For having fcap'd the Tavern fo,
There never was a greater Foe,
Encounter'd yet by *Pompey*, No
                    Nor *Cæfar*.

A Conftable both ftern and dread,
Who is from Muftard, Brooms and Thread,
Preferr'd to be the Brainlefs Head ---
                    O' th' People,

A

A Gown 'had on by Age made gray,
A Hat too, which as Folk do fay,
Is firnam'd to this very day

        A Steeple ;

His Staff, which knew as well as he,
The Bus'nefs of Authority,
Stood bolt upright at fight of me ;

        Very true 'tis,

Thofe louzy Currs that hither come
To keep the King's Peace fafe at home,
Yet cannot keep the Vermin from

        Their *Cutis.*

Stand ! ftand ! fayes one, and come before ---
You lye, faid I, like a Son of a Whore,
I can't, nor will not ftand, --- that's more ---

        D'ye mutter ?

          You

You watchful Knaves, I'll tell what,
Yond' Officer i'th May-pole Hat,
I'll make as drunk as any Rat,
                          Or Otter.

The Conſtable began to ſwell,
Altho' he lik'd the motion well :
Quoth he, my Friend, this I muſt tell
                          Ye clearly,

The Peſtilence you can't forget,
Nor the Diſpute with *Dutch,* nor yet
The dreadful Fire, that made us get
                          Up early.

From which, quoth he, this I infer,
To have a Body's Conſcience clear,
Excelleth any coſtly cheer,
                          Or Banquets ;
                                    Beſides,

Befides, (and 'faith I think he wept)
Were it not better you had kept
Within your Chamber, and have flept

> In Blanquets :

But I'll advife you by and by,
A Pox of all advife, faid I,
Your Janizaries look as dry

> As *Vulcan* :

Come, here's a fhilling, fetch it in,
We come not now to talk of Sin,
Our Bus'nefs muft be to begin

> A full Can.

At laft, I made the Watch-men drunk,
Examin'd here and there a Punk,
And then away to Bed I flunk

> To hide it,

> > God

God fave the Queen, ---- but as for you,

Who will thefe Dangers not efchew,

I'd have you all go home and fpue

                    As I did.

The Lawyers Demurrer *argued.*

*By the Loyal ADDRESSERS (the Gentlemen)
of* Grays-Inne, *againft an ORDER made by
the Bench of the faid Society.*

To the Tune of *Packington's* Pound, Or,
    The Round-head Reviv'd.

I.

DEar Friends, and good People, with Gowns,
    and with none ;

I'll tell you a Tale of a parcel of *Whiggs,*

The Spawn of fome *Rebells* in year Forty One,

Who, like their damn'd Sires, purfue their Intrigues:

                    It

It occasions amazing,

That some Members of *Grays Inn*, (Raising:

Turn Tail to their King, from whom they'd their.

You Mortals of Law be confounded for ever,

Who refuse an Address made to your Law-giver.

II.

By a musty old Custom, call'd Order of Pension.

Giving Thanks to the King was judg'd an Affray,

And straight they Decreed, 'twas just to Dis-
bench One, *(S)*

For shewing himself more Loyal than they :

So thus the *Dom. Com.*

Speak loudly for some, (Mum.

But propose the King's Int'rest the word shall be

You Mortals of Law be confounded for ever;

Who refuse an Address made to your Law-giver.

III.

III.

Men of the Sword they fay make a Divifion, (*S*)
· And militant Lawyers their Wifdoms difown,
So that from the King to have had a Commiffion,
Does not confift with a tatter'd old Gown :
   Thefe men make pretence,
   Both to Law and to Senfe,   (Prince,
Yet fay the Law's broke, if you fight for your
   Tou Mortals of Law be confounded for ever,
   Who refufe an Addrefs made to your Law-giver.

IV.

          (out,
From th' Ancients (they urge) this Order comes
And therefore expect a ready Obedience,
But how can that be, fince their Mafterfhips doat,
And they themfelves have forgotten Allegiance:
   Therefore let's pray,
   Both by Night and by Day,
That they may Conform, and then we'll Obey.
           Tou

You Mortals of Law be confounded for ever,
Who refuse an Address made to your Law-giver.

V.

But wou'd it not move a Heart made of Flint,
To think that a House must continue no longer,
Since the grave Gubernators refus'd to consent,
Except 'twere propos'd by a Bar-Iron-monger; (C)
    Or else by a Brewer,   (O)
      Who serves them with Beer,
So small, that they'r fill'd with Suspicion and Fear.
    You Mortals of Law be confounded for ever;
    Who refuse an Address made to your Law-giver.

VI.

Now some of the younger disconsolate fry, (G)
As if they'd been still at --- *Quæso Magister,*
Under such strange Apprehensions did lye,
They desir'd to consult the Chappel-Minister;

One

One of the young men,
Wou'ld not handle a Pen,
For my Lord and my Father won't take me agen.
You Mortals of Law be confounded for ever,
Who refuse an Address made to your Law-giver.

VII.

The number of those who refus'd to subscribe,
Are fitly compar'd to the days of Poor *Job*,
Few and Evil ---and of a Satanical Tribe,
Who scandalize all the rest of the Robe ;
Those of the Bar-mess,
Who cry'd---No Address,
Found their Party of Faction were two to one less.
You Mortals of Law be confounded for ever,
Who refuse an Address made to your Law-giver.

VIII.

VIII.

Now you have heard of thefe *Lawyers Demurrer*,
And how their weak Arguments are over-rul'd,
Without all Difpute, will think an *Abhorrer*,
Of them and Petitions, are loyally bold.
    For fuch Impudence,
    Both at Bar and at Bench,
Proceeds from thofe Men who their King would
    Retrench;
    You mortals of Law be confounded for ever,
    Who refufe an Addrefs made to your Law-giver.

The SWORD's *Farewell, upon the approach of a* Michaelmas Term.

HEalth to my Friends, a terror to my Foes,
   Revenging Wrongs, impatient of blows,
Couragious Metal, trueſt of all Steels,
Sure to thy Maſter, always at his heels;
Ready to jog him by the Elbow, when
He is confronted by the Sons of Men.
Soul of my Weapon, thou ſhalt take thy Reſt;
And acquieſce within thy Sable Neſt,
One Month muſt fix thee in a certain Station,
Thy Maſter's *Term* muſt prove thine own *Vacation*
Till that's expir'd (his Honour be thy Pawn)
Though here thour't hang'd yet thou ſhalt not l
                    (draw
Thou ſhalt not now too late at Night appear,
T'incenſe the King's Almighty Officer,
Nor vex his Watch, leſt by his great Command
They knock thy Maſter down, and bid him ſtand

Nor fly at Mortal wight, though ne're fo tall,
Who paffing by Surrenders not the Wall,
Nor pufh at Bayliffs ftout denouncing War :
We know no Sergeants now but at the Bar.
They're fix'd (but with fuch moveable devotion,)
Come when you will, you'l find them in a Motion·
Not willing any Man fhould be oppreft,
'Tis only *Judgment* that they would Arreft.
Thou fhalt not now be bare, when *Hector* cloaths,
And backs the Lye with rags of fwelling Oaths,
Now fuch great words admit a Period,
He muft fpeak only truth, *fo help him God*;
The Stile is chang'd, (the Seafon fo will have it)
If he will fwear, 't muft be by *Affidavit*.

Thou muft not now come forth in view, as once,
To fright a Rev'rend Bawd, and build a Sconce,
Nor make a Drawer ftand all Night to Skink
Full cups, and watch to fill thy Mafter Drink,
To rubifie his Cheeks, though when he will,
He can take out a *Fieri Facias* ftill.

Or Prefidents (if common Writs do fail,)
Direct to me a fpecial Writ of *Aile.*

(Whilom at such a Sign conven'd the Wits;
But now no Sign is known except for Writs)
Thou must forbear a while at *Inn* and *Inn*,
T' out-brave whom thou suspecteft like to win:
No jogging chance must now blind mortal Eyes,
We'll find fresh Bail of *Men* and not of *Dice*,
Pray for an Action now, and not an *Ace*,
Let every *Deuce* produce a Debtor's case:
And in the stead of every *Trey* that's thrown,
So many *Tryals* may we call our own.
To cast a *Quatre* now we must forget,
And call to mind a *Quare Impedit*.
Each *Cinque* a *Capias*, and for every *Size*
Wish that a *Scire Facias* may arise.
Now we must think *Hazard* brings little gain,
Throw a *Mandamus* rather than a *Main* ;
On certainties 'tis safest to rely,
More's gain'd by *Bill*, than gotten by the *By*.
To *Play-Houses* thou now shalt bid adieu,
Although the Farce be gay enough and new,
Ne're before acted, brings thee not among
Those that fell Two and Six-pence for a Song.

No

No Idle Scenes fit bufie times as thefe,
Inftead of Playes we now converfe with Pleas ;
And 't's thought the laft do favour more of Wit,
For thofe have Plots to fpend, but thefe to get.
   (Give way, Great *Shakefpear*, and immortal *Ben*,
To *Doe* and *Roe*, *John Den* and *Richard Fen*.)
Farewel(dear Sword)thour't prov'd, and laid afide;
Thy youngeft Brother, *Penknife*, muft be try'd ;
That thou art beft, needs but a thin difpute,
Thou woundeft skin of *Man*, he skin of *Brute*;
'Tis pity fuch an Urchin long fhould reign
To raze a Line, when thou can'ft prick a Vein.
'Tis thou can'ft make fuch horrid bloody work
Will fright the Pope, and fcare the biggeft *Turk* ;
Thy very name will make a Cripple run
Swift as a Courtier from a City Dunn.
   Now *Tom* (in Acres rich, is come to Town)
To change the Title of a Yeoman's Son,
Thou bid'ft him kneel, and ftroak'ft his empty Skul,
And mak'ft him rife *Sir Thomas* Worfhipful:
Thus thou mak'ft fpecial Knights of common men
When he hath made his beft 'tis but a Pen;

                             Yet

Yet fuch a Pen, that when't has learn't it's Trade,
It may undo the Knight which thou haft made.
   That thou art monftrous valiant is too certain,
For inftance this, in fine (as faith Sir *Martin*)
Th'haft kill'd---But foft, fome wifer are than fome,
I fhould *Marr-all* if I difcover whom.
In point of Honour this, (deny't who can)
Thou never turn'dft thy *Back* to any Man:
The fhort and long on't's thus, I'll fafely fay,
                  (run away :
Though thou fhould'ft *break*, thou would'ft not
Yet 'twould not wound thy credit long, for when
The *Term* is done, I'll fet thee up agen.

Cedant ARma togæ, concedat laurea linguæ.

Wrote

Wrote in the Banquetting-Houſe in Grayes-Inn-Walks.

HERE Damſel ſits diſconſolate,
   Curſing the Rigor of her Fate,
Till Squire Inſipid having ſpy'd her,
Takes Heart of Grace, and ſquats beſide her.
   He thus accoſts, ---- Madam, By Gad
You are at once both fair and ſad.
She innocently does ſubmit
To all the Tyrants of his Wit.
The Bargain's made, ſhe firſt is led
To the three Tuns, and ſo to Bed.

But yonder comes a graver Fop,
With heavy Shoe, and Boot-hoſe-top;
To him repairs a virtuous Sir,
Whoſe Queſtion is, What News does ſtir?
With Face askrew, he then declares
The probability of Wars :

                         And

And gives an ample satisfaction
Of *English*, *French*, and *Dutch* Transaction.
Thus chattering out three houres Tale,
They tread to th' Mag-pye, to drink Ale.

Death and the old man.

A Paraphrase upon one of Æsop's Fables.

A Poor old man, who had by cleaving wood,
 Full threescore years procur'd a livelihood;
He never ran the various risques of Fate,
Each day his shoulders bore an equal weight,
Till now at last of Age he did complain,
And thought each Load did weigh as much again.
 One Evening coming home he made a stop,
And wanting strength, he let his burden drop ;
Then sate upon it, with a proud neglect.
And ner'e till now did on himself reflect.
 What Being's this call'd Man, and what am I ?
One of the Drudges of Mortality.

I've

I've cut down Wood enough, now Death attend,
And to my Life and Labour put an end :
With that the Grifly Skelleton appear'd,
And the old man was from his Senfes fcar'd :
  Quoth Death, Old fellow, if you'd fpeak with me,
I'le give a period to your mifery :
Oh No, fweet Sir, quoth the amazed Grandfire,
I wifh it not, as I'me a living man Sir ;
I only did defire, becaufe I'me weak,
And cannot lift this Burthen to my Neck,
That you'ld be pleas'd, to lend a helping hand,
And I am yours, *hereafter*, to command.

Moral.

Silly old wretch, who living art oppreſt,
Yet dar'ſt not venture on Eternal reſt.

Upon

Upon the *Death of* Edward Story, Efq; *Mafter of the* Pond, *and Principal of* Bernards-Inn.

(drown'd,

LET all that read thefe Lines in Tears be
 Since *Story's* dead, the Mafter of the *Pond*;
What idle Tales fantaftick Poets feign
About God *Neptune*, and his ftormy Main,
That his Dominion's great, 'tis no fuch matter,
What great Command can there be over Water?
To *Story's* power 'twere Non-fence to compare it,
For he was Mafter of a *Pond* of *Claret*:
And he this Scarlet *Sea*, like *Mofes*, --- did
To all his Club of *Ifraelites* divide:
And when too late at night fome came in doz'd,
The *Pond* o'er them, as o'er th' *Egyptians* clos'd.
 This *Pond* was *Helicon*, where *Story* fate
Like mighty *Phœbus*, in his Chair of State:
His Tongue made Mufick like *Apollo's* Lyre,
Which when he us'd, he filenc'd, all the Quire;
He had his Mufes too, but more than Nine,
Befides, they're of the Gender Mafculine:

Of

Of different Subjects every Mufe did fing, (bring.
Which they from *Johns*, or *Grays-Inn* Walks did
Some Foreign Matters fang, another Mufe,
In humble Stile, fang of Domeftick News;
Some fang of bloody Plots againft the Throne
And Government; another fang of none;
Till by fome fign his pleafure was expreft,
Then all were quiet while he told a Jeft.

And as this witty Club he kept in awe,
He headed too, a Body of the Law;
Yet for all that, as skilful as he was,
Death brought his *Action* without fhewing *Caufe*.
And ran him to the *Utlary* with fuch fpeed,
He had not time enough to fuperfede.
　With all Mankind *Death* muft his *Intereft* clear,
　But to call in the *Principle*'s fevere.

Upon the Memory of Mr. John Sprat, *late Steward of* Grayes-Inn.

CAN any man in reason think it fit
   That Death should eat a *Steward* at a Bit?
And in *one long Vacation* should devour,
What, in all Conscience, might have serv'd for *four?*
Had it been *Term-time* he'd have taken course
To have repell'd both him and all his Force.
Villanous Death ! he would have plac'd a Chop
With every Dart that thou haft in thy Shop:
Thou durst not then attempt him (meager Glutton)
When he and's men were arm'd with *Beef* & *Mutton*;
Thou wert afraid to nibble at *John Sprat*
While *Barrel-Cod* and *Whiting* were in date ;
His Voice disbanded thee, and all thy Troop,
When gracefully he gave the word, *Serve up.*
'Twas cowardly to take him, when *Raw Fruits,*
When *Turneps, Cucumbers,* and *Cabbedge Roots*
Had chill'd his Blood, he had defi'd being sick,
Had he surviv'd the time they call *Tres Mich'.*

                    But

But why had not thy hungry Maw been eas'd,
If *Tasborough* or *Taylor* thou hadſt ſeiz'd;
Thoſe *ſingle parts* of *Middle-piece* and *Rump*,
Inſatiate thou! to fall upon the *Chump.*
Since *buſie Sprat* (our lives Truſtee) is dead,
The *Bottled* Joyes of *Norfolk* too are fled:
The *Thetford-Ale*, which won the hearts of Youth,
And made them chant his praiſe with open mouth:
Whom afterwards he'd greet in friendly ſort,
Your Chamber, Sir, I think's in Concy Court.
When will't be opportune---- to bring my Bill ?
D'ſlife, ne'r talk of that man ; when you will.
Then he (good man) who alwayes knew his time,
To Chamber-door would in the Morning clime.

Now truſty Sprat is gone, there will not come
So Generous a Steward in his Room:
He would in *Younger Brothers* ſtill confide:
Whoſe Parents do in Foreign Lands reſide:
He entertain'd them well ; yet did not know
Whether their Friends were living there or no.
They ſcorn'd to come as *Commoners* to eat,
But took it as the *Noble Steward's Treat.*

Ah,

Ah cruel Hag! (though Muse be out of breath,
Yet see! she'l have one parting-blow at Death)
Were there not equal Standers of the Hall,
That thou didst call *Sprat* in a *private Call* ?
And, which is worse, by Tyrannous permission
He did go out before he did *petition.*
Some Presidents 'tis likely we shall find
Upon the Roll of *Commons* left behind ;
Which his *surviving* Friends (without a *Bribe,*
It is believ'd) are willing to transcribe:
Therefore 'tis hop'd (lest *Youth* should be perple:
That his *Executors* may *Go out* next.

His Epitaph.

BEneath this Stone, Reader, there lieth flat
Upon his Back the trusty *Steward Sprat* :
Disturb him not, for if he chance to stir,
He'll say, *When shall I wait upon you, Sir ?*

FINIS.